The Promissory

KYIRIS ASHLEY

URBAN AINT DEAD

P.O Box 448

Maybrook, NY 12543

Cover Design: Akirecover2cover.com

Edited By: Shawna Brim / Ladies of Lit

URBAN AINT DEAD and coinciding logo(s) are registered properties.

Contact Author on FB: Kyiris Ashley / IG: @Kyiris_Ashley / TikTok: @Kyiris _Ashley/ Email: KyirisAshley@gmail.com

Contact Publisher at www.urbanaintdead.com

Email: urbanaintdead@gmail.com

Print ISBN: 979-8-9908882-7-2

Stay Up to Date

To stay up to date on new releases, plus get information on contests,
sneak peeks and more,

Click the link below...
https://mailchi.mp/6d21003686d1/subscribe

Soundtracks

Scan the QR Code below to listen to the Soundtracks/Singles of some of your favorite U.A.D titles:

Don't have Spotify or Apple Music?
No Sweat!
Visit your choice streaming platform and search URBAN AINT
DEAD.

Currently on lock serving a bid?
JPay, iHeartRadio, WHATEVER!
We got you covered.
Simply log into your facility's kiosk or tablet, go to music and search
URBAN AINT DEAD.

U.A.D PRESENTS

Like & Follow us on social media:

FB - URBAN AINT DEAD

IG: @uadpresents

Tik Tok - @uadpresents

Submission Guidelines

Submit the first three chapters of your completed manuscript to urbanaintdead@gmail.com, subject line: Your book's title. The manuscript must be in a .doc file and sent as an attachment. The document should be in Times New Roman, double-spaced, and in size 12 font. Also, provide your synopsis and full contact information. If sending multiple submissions, they must each be in a separate email. Have a story but no way to submit it electronically? You can still submit to URBAN AINT DEAD. Send in the first three chapters, written or typed, of your completed manuscript to:

URBAN AINT DEAD
P.O Box 448
Maybrook, NY 12543

DO NOT send original manuscript. Must be a duplicate.
Provide your synopsis and a cover letter containing your full contact information.
Thanks for considering URBAN AINT DEAD.

NOTE FROM THE AUTHOR

This is a dark romance novel. Read at your own risk. It gets extremely dark and nasty in Banks' world, and if you enter, you must be just as dark and nasty as he is. This is your chance to grab yourself a towel because if you begin this book, you're going to need it. If you make it to the next page after this warning, I have no choice but to assume you like to play with the big dawgs. In that case, I welcome you to A'zir "Banks" McFarland's world, where you will soon be a part of the Banks' Navy.

Chapter One

BRAYLEN

I looked at the clock on the wall and smiled. I had fifteen minutes left in my shift, and I couldn't wait to get off work. As a lead line worker at Ford Motor Company, I was a part of the Big Three in the auto industry. If you were from Detroit, chances were either you or your spouse worked for either Ford, Chrysler, or GM. I'd been working twelve-hour shifts for the past six days and was ready to go home. My body ached, and all I wanted was a hot bubble bath and a glass of wine. I waited patiently for the clock to read five, knowing that once I clocked out, I would be on vacation for an entire week.

The truth was that I hated working so many hours, but with rent as high as it was and bills that were piling up, I knew I didn't have a choice. Thankfully, my vacation would be paid, so I wouldn't be missing out on any money that I couldn't afford to lose. As soon as the clock hit five, I was on my way to the break room to grab my belongings and clock out. The moment I got into my car, my phone rang. I closed my door and started the ignition before answering the call through my Bluetooth.

"Bitch, it's five fifteen on Friday. It's ninety-two degrees. I ain't got no nigga, so the others can trick on me," Vita, my best friend, chanted into the phone, putting her own little twist on Glorilla's lyrics.

"Girl, you crazy. What you up to?"

"Shit, just seein' if you was tryna go out tonight. I feel like shakin' this ass."

"Bitch, that's a whole lotta ass to be shakin'," I joked.

Vita was what the men would call thick as hell. However, she didn't lay on a table for the curves she had. Vita came from a long line of thick women, with her grandmother having an ass so big you could fit a Sunday dinner on top of it. Vita stayed in the gym, making sure to keep her waistline small. She stood five foot three inches tall with smooth dark chocolate skin. She had long, honey blond locs that were always twisted and styled to perfection. Vita had been my best friend since the seventh grade.

Vita had been there for me when nobody else had. She was my therapist, my right hand, my sister, my best friend, and my go to when times were both good and bad. She was the type of friend that everyone needed but not everyone had. Vita would ride for me with no questions asked, and in return, I would do the same for her. If ever Vita needed anything, I would always be the first to lend a helping hand.

"And you betta know it! These bitches out here laying on tables to get the ass my mama gave me at birth. It's only right that I shake this muthafucka. Anyway, what you doing?"

"Shit, just leaving work. 'Bout to go home and see what's up with Kyrie. I don't know about going out. I gotta see if he has something planned for us to do tonight. You know I started my vacation today, so he might want to do something."

"Girl, you know Kyrie ass ain't planning shit, and if he is, you gon' be the one paying for it. You might as well go out with me and let some fine ass niggas buy us drinks."

No matter how much Vita loved me, she never accepted Kyrie as my husband. Six months into our relationship, Vita caught him walking into a hotel with another woman. She immediately called me and let me know what she'd seen. Without a second thought, I got into my car and drove from the east side of Detroit to Dearborn in fifteen minutes, doing a hundred down both 94 and the Southfield freeways. When I arrived, I met Vita in the lobby, and she walked me up to their room.

Placing my hand over the peephole, I knocked on the door before putting on the most pleasant voice I could muster and calling out housekeeping. Just as I suspected, the door opened, and Vita and I barged inside. The shocked expression on Kyrie's face let me know he was caught. When I looked over to the bed and saw the naked woman lying there, I lost it, grabbing and swinging punches at Kyrie. Tears fell from my eyes with each punch I threw. I couldn't believe Kyrie was cheating on me. I thought we were happy.

Before I knew it, Kyrie grabbed me up and threw me against the wall, causing me to fall to the floor. Vita was instantly on his ass, punching him so hard that he stumbled back, giving me time to stand to my feet.

"How the fuck could you do this to me, Kyrie? You over here giving dick to random bitches in a hotel room?" Without allowing him to answer, I punched him so hard in his eye that he fell to the floor.

"Get yo hands off my man!" the woman yelled before charging at me.

She grabbed my hair, pulling me down before slapping me in my face. When Vita saw me and the girl fighting, she let go of Kyrie and began beating the shit out of the girl. We were both so focused on fighting the girl that none of us noticed Kyrie as he grabbed his belongings and made his way out the hotel room. The next thing I knew, Dearborn police were entering the room, breaking up the fight and handcuffing us all. After spending a night in jail, Vita couldn't help but tell me how she hoped I never fucked with Kyrie again. Needless to say, he apologized, and I fell for it. But Vita wasn't having it, not wanting to have anything to do with him from that day forward.

"Nah, I'm good. If Kyrie found out I was letting some other niggas buy me drinks, he would have a damn fit. You know how that nigga is. He don't play about other niggas talkin' to his wife."

"Who give a fuck what he thinks? That nigga can't buy you nothing. Everything you got you have to get yourself, and on top of that, the nigga be gambling all y'all money away. I honestly don't know what you see in that nigga. The only reason he don't want no other niggas talkin' to you is cause he scared you gon' realize it's someone better out there for you," Vita confessed.

"Damn, tell me how you really feel. I get you don't like Kyrie and all, but he's my husband. So, when you talkin' to me, you will respect him. Our relationship is not for you or anybody else to understand. I'm just gon' call you back, Vita."

"Now don't be like that. We can go out and have a good time tonight. It's no need for you to be getting all in your feelings."

"I'ma just call you back." With that, I ended the call and continued to drive home. A part of me was only mad because I knew Vita was right. Kyrie and I had been married for the past five years, getting married when I was only twenty, and our lives had never been perfect. Kyrie had a gambling problem, which usually resulted in him losing all our money, forcing me to work overtime just to make ends meet. There were times I would even have to hide money at Vita's house just to ensure Kyrie didn't gamble all the bill money away. I truly loved my husband; however, I wished he would change his ways. Pulling up to the townhouse I shared with him, I parked in my usual parking spot before getting out my car and walking to the door. The moment I opened it, I could hear Kyrie on the phone.

"I just need a few more days... I won't have it by tomorrow... I just need an extension." He paused for a moment, listening to the person on the other end of the phone speak before he continued. "Okay, I'll see you tomorrow."

"Is everything okay?" I asked, walking up closer to him.

"Huh? Um, yeah, I'm good. Why you say that?"

"I mean, the conversation you were just havin' on the phone didn't sound like everything was good, so I'm just makin' sure."

"Well, if you wasn't eavesdroppin' on my conversation, then you wouldn't have to ask me no questions like that."

Before I could say another word, Kyrie stormed off, rushing upstairs. *What the fuck just happened?* I thought to myself, shaking my head before taking a seat on the light gray sofa in my living room. A few minutes later, Kyrie was walking back downstairs, letting me know he was leaving and needed the keys to my car. He didn't even give me time to answer. Instead, he grabbed my keys from the coffee table and walked out the house. *Damn, well, what the fuck was all that about?*

Standing from the couch, I walked into my kitchen and grabbed a bottle of wine and a glass before making my way upstairs. There was no telling what time Kyrie would be back, but I knew he didn't have anything planned for us to do tonight. I ran myself a hot bath before pouring vanilla scented bubble bath into the water. Removing my work clothes, I looked at myself in the mirror.

"Damn, I wish I would have never stopped working out." I spoke aloud to myself.

Although I wasn't sloppy, I'd gained a few unwanted pounds to my once toned body. Before I'd married Kyrie, I was in the gym every other day. However, after we'd gotten married, he expressed to me that he didn't want me in the gym half naked in front of all the men that could be looking at me. Being newly married, I didn't want to disobey my husband, so I agreed and stopped working out at the gym. My once six pack abs had turned into a small pupa. My thighs and arms were not as toned as they once were either, and the cellulite was starting to appear.

I wasn't fat, but as I looked at myself in the mirror, I knew that I would be if I didn't hurry up and get back into the gym. I ran my hand over my shoulder length, dark brown hair that I now kept in a ponytail. It had been years since I'd gotten my hair professionally done. There was a time when I was at the salon every week, getting my hair styled to perfection. That was until Kyrie began gambling our money away. Now, we barely had enough money to pay the bills, let alone for weekly hair appointments.

Running my hand over my caramel complected skin, I noticed the bags that had formed underneath my dark brown, almond shaped eyes. It was the first time I'd realized I'd become a shell of my former self. The dream of a wonderful married life had become a nightmare as I realized just how unhappy I actually was. Pouring myself a glass of wine, I eased down into the hot bubbly water as I took a sip from my glass. Not wanting to spend another Friday night at home, I decided that I would take Vita up on her offer and go out.

Once I was out the tub, I oiled my body before heading into my room and opening my closet. After about fifteen minutes of browsing through my clothes, I finally decided on a pair of black leggings and a black lace bustier. I brushed my hair back into a neat ponytail, my signature style, before applying light makeup to my face. Once I finished getting dressed, I finished my look off with a pair of gold hoop earrings and a gold necklace. I sprayed myself with Into The Stars by Bath and Body Works and was ready to go. Making my way down to my living room, I sat on the couch, sipping a glass of wine, while I waited on Vita.

Chapter Two

KYRIE

I pulled into the driveway of the small brick house which belonged to my homeboy, Jason's mother. He'd been living in his mother's basement since his wife kicked him out of the house almost a year ago. Grabbing my phone from the cup holder of Braylen's Honda Accord, I shot a text to Jason, letting him know I was outside. A few moments later, the front door opened, and I got out the car and walked inside.

"What up doe, bro? Why you look like you just lost yo dog?" Jason asked the moment I walked through the door.

"Man, fuck a dog. I'm about to lose my fuckin' life. I owe Banks a hundred thousand dollars that I don't fuckin' have. He told me that if I didn't pay him by tomorrow, he would kill me. Fuck, man! I done really fucked up this time." I shook my head, finally realizing my mistake.

"Why the fuck would you borrow a hundred thousand from Banks, and what the fuck did you do with the money? I ain't tryna be funny, but from where I stand, it don't look like you ever had that much money."

Jason pointed to the nappy cornrows in my head that looked like they were a day away from turning to locs. I hadn't had my hair braided in months, but when I brushed them and put on a durag to tie them down, they didn't look so bad. However, I guess nobody else saw it that way. The Walmart jeans I wore were about two sizes too big, so I tied a shoestring around them to hold them up. I also wore a plain white shirt and a three-year-old pair of white Nike Air Force Ones.

"Jason, man, now is not the time for jokes. I'm in some deep shit. What the fuck am I going to do?"

"Shit, who's joking? You don't look like you touched that much money ever in life. You wear the same pair of jeans every time I see you. Nigga, you don't even own a belt."

"These my favorite pants, and I do got a belt. I just don't know where it is. Now are you gon' clown me or help me? Because it's the help that I need," I replied, not liking where the conversation was going.

"Relax, I think I might have a solution to all of this. My mama knows this old lady that lives in one of them big ass houses in West Bloomfield. She lives all by herself in this big ass house and don't have no family. My mama sits with her once a week, just to keep her company. Anyway, my mama left something over the lady's house last week, and I rode with her to get it. I remember the address."

"Okay, so you remember the address. You think this old lady just gon' give me a hundred thousand dollars just because I need it?"

"Nigga, we gon' take it along with whatever else we see up in that muthafucka. That old bitch is rich as fuck, and she on her way outta here anyway. We can take what we need and be good off that shit."

"When can we go?" I asked. I knew I didn't have any time to waste if I wanted to stay alive. Seeing this as my only option, I knew it was something that had to be done.

"We can go tonight. I just want to wait until she goes to sleep. I'm not tryin' to hurt anyone, just take her shit and get some money. Once she asleep, this shit gon' be easy."

So, that was exactly what we did, waiting until eleven that night before making our way from Detroit to West Bloomfield, ready to take the valuables of a defenseless old woman. Pulling onto the street when GPS informed me, I turned off the headlights before pulling up to the massive home.

"Damn, she lives in this muthafucka all by herself?" I asked, looking over at the home in disbelief.

The house was a huge brick mansion with huge picture windows that allowed you to see right inside the home. There was an island in the middle of the circular driveway which housed a water fountain, and all the grass was neatly trimmed. The house was beautiful, and I couldn't help but smile, knowing I was about to get all the money I needed.

"Yeah, she never had any kids, and all her family died. It's just her." Jason reached into his pocket and pulled out two pairs of black gloves before handing a pair over to me.

I slid the gloves onto my hands before grabbing a black hoodie from the backseat. Putting it over my skinny frame, I placed the hood over my head to conceal my face. I stood five foot eight and a hundred forty-five pounds. With no facial hair or tattoos to identify me, I knew I would be able to blend in as long as I didn't come face to face with anyone. It was dark outside, and we were both dressed in all black. I couldn't believe this shit had just fallen into my hands. This was the perfect heist.

"You ready?" I asked, looking over at Jason.

"Fuck yeah, let's get it."

With that, we both got out of the car and hurriedly made our way up the lawn and around to the side of the house. Jason's mother had told him a number of times how the little old woman never remembered to lock her side door. We hoped that tonight would be a night she didn't remember. We made our way to the door, praying it would be unlocked, and fortunately for us, it was. Opening the door, we both stepped into the house, quietly closing the door behind us. We walked through the house, looking around for anything of value. Making our way up the grand staircase, we came across a room filled with fur coats, expensive clothes, and jewelry.

"We done hit the fuckin' jackpot," Jason whispered, walking over to the glass case that was filled with diamond jewelry.

Immediately, I began going through all the drawers, looking for whatever it was that I wanted to take with me. When I came across an envelope filled with one-hundred-dollar bills, my eyes lit up. Looking over my shoulder to see Jason going through drawers and not paying attention to me, I quickly stuffed the envelope into the pocket of my hoodie before I continued looking through the drawers.

Five minutes later, we were running back to the car and pulling off down the street, headed back to Jason's house. Jason informed me that he would take the jewelry to the pawn shop as soon as it opened in the morning and would call me when he had the money. Agreeing, I dropped Jason off before pulling off down the street, already having my own plan to make the money I needed. Getting onto I-94, I made my way downtown, heading to Motor City Casino.

Pulling into the parking structure, I parked before pulling the envelop from my pocket and counting the money. It was twenty-five thousand dollars. Although it wasn't nearly as much as I needed to pay back Banks, I knew I could take it into the casino and make the money quickly. With that, I got out of the car and made my way into the casino, ready to do what I did best – gamble.

Walking directly to the Blackjack table, I took a seat before placing five thousand dollars on the table, buying my first set of chips. I placed bet after bet, and within six hours, I was up a hundred and ten thousand dollars. Knowing this was the money I needed to save my life; I did something I'd never done before. I left the table and went to cash out. I stood in line as I waited to walk up to the teller. I couldn't help but smile at the fact that all my problems were now over.

By the time I made it back to my car, it was almost seven in the morning. Pulling out my phone, I placed a call to Banks. I knew it was early, and he might not even be up, but I was so excited that I could finally pay him back that I didn't care. Banks answered the phone on the second ring, and I immediately let him know he could pick up his money.

"I'll be home in about thirty minutes," I confirmed.

"Alright, I'll meet you there. Oh, and Kyrie, this bet not be a game. If you don't have my money when I pull up, you know what's gon' happen."

"I got it, and it's all there. I'll see you in thirty."

Knowing Braylen would be upset that I stayed out all night, I decided to make a stop before going back home. Knowing I needed something to put a smile on my wife's face, I pulled into the parking lot of a Kroger not too far from our house. Not wanting to leave my money in the car, I placed it all in the backpack I kept in the backseat of Braylen's car. Swinging the backpack over my shoulder, I got out the car and made my way inside the store, heading straight to the flower section. I was on such a natural high that I hadn't noticed I'd been followed since I left the casino.

I picked out two bouquets of flowers before going to the candy section and picking out a box of chocolates. Rushing up to the register,

I paid for the items before leaving the store. I'd just made it to the car when I heard someone calling out to me. At first, I wasn't going to answer, but when the man called out to me again, I decided to see what he wanted. When I turned to answer the man, two men rushed at me. One punched me in the face so hard that I fell to the ground instantly. The two men immediately began kicking and stomping me, making it impossible for me to defend myself. Before I knew it, the guys were running away with my backpack and the flowers and the candy I'd just purchased for Braylen.

Slowly standing to my feet, I doubled over, praying my ribs weren't broken. I looked around, but the two men had left as quickly as they came. Getting into my car, I headed home the same way I'd left – broke. The moment I pulled up to the townhome I shared with Braylen and saw Banks' black Cadillac Escalade parked out front, I couldn't do anything but shake my head. I knew it was over. I'd called Banks over to pick up money that I now didn't have. I watched as Banks got out of his SUV and walked over to my car. He wore a dark gray suit and looked to be a normal businessman; however, there was nothing normal about the business that Banks did. I slowly got out the car as I thought about what I was going to tell him. Not coming up with a better idea than the truth, I started talking.

"Banks, I had your money. I swear I did. But I just got robbed while I was on my way home. As you can see, they beat the shit outta me then took all the money I'd just made. But I swear I just need a day or two, and I'll have it for you. I promise. I came into so..."

Before I could finish my statement, Banks motioned to the two men that were sitting inside his SUV. Two tall men that were dressed in black suits walked over to us. They grabbed me up forcefully and threw me into the backseat of the SUV.

"Come on, Banks. Please don't do this. I'm telling you I just need two more days. I can have you straight by then," I pleaded.

"I came here to collect money you told me you had, only to get here and you don't have it. The games are over. You can't pay up, then you know what that means." Without another word, the door was closed, and the SUV pulled out the parking lot.

A few moments later, we pulled up to an abandoned warehouse, and I was pulled from the SUV by Banks' goons. They dragged me into the warehouse, tossing me down onto the plastic covered floor. I looked around in fear, already knowing what was next. This nigga was about to kill me, and there was nothing I could do about it. I watched in fear as Banks took his suit jacket off, revealing the huge muscles in his arms. Unbuttoning the cuffs of his sleeves, he rolled them up to his elbows. He grabbed a crowbar from the plastic square table that set in the middle of the warehouse. Walking up to me slowly, Banks swung the crowbar before it landed on my back.

"Ahh!" I screamed out in pain each time the crowbar hit my body, instantly bruising my skin.

Banks hit me several more times, blood spattering onto the thick plastic. If my ribs weren't broken when I was robbed, they for damn sure were broken now. Once he was tired of beating me, Banks ordered his goons to tie me to a chair. I pleaded, hoping Banks would listen; however, my pleads fell on deaf ears. The two goons picked me up, each grabbing one of my arms, before dragging me to the chair.

"Come on, Banks, please. You really don't have to do this. Please just give me a couple more days. All I gotta do is go get some more money, and I can have it back to you in no time. I already got some shit lined up." I knew that once Jason took the jewelry to the pawn shop, I would have a little money to work with. I figured I could take it to the casino and turn it into the money I needed. *Shit, if I did it before, I can do it again.*

"You had your chance to give me my money, and you fucked that up. Now, you have to see what happens to muthafuckas that think they can play with me."

Banks signaled to one of his goons, and he walked to the other side of the room, grabbing a chainsaw, before bringing it back over to Banks. Banks turned it on and slowly walked up to me.

"Come on, man, please. I'll do anything. I'll take you with me to get the money. We can go together. Just please, Banks, don't do this."

Banks said nothing as he continued toward me. Sweat pooled under my armpits, soaking my shirt as I prayed Banks would just listen to me. However, nothing I said stopped Banks from coming toward me. For Banks, it wasn't about the money anymore. It was about his respect. We had an agreement, and I had forfeited that. Nothing I could say now would make Banks change his mind. I'd played with his money, and for that, I would pay up with my life.

I watched in horror as Banks inched closer to me with the buzzing chainsaw in his hands. I knew it was the end, and all I could do was think back on my life and all the many ways I'd fucked it up. I knew every lie and wrongdoing was now catching up to me. This was how I would die, and there was nothing I could do to stop it. As I closed my eyes, not wanting to witness my fate, I took one last attempt to save my life.

"Wait, what about my wife? Would you take her? She's worth way more than a hundred thousand. You can keep her for a night."

With those words, Banks stopped in his tracks, looking at me in confusion. "What did you just say to me?"

"I said you can take my wife for a night. She will do anything you need, and that will be my payment," I confirmed.

"A night? Nah, that ain't shit. If you selling her for a hundred thousand, then I'm gon' have her for a week."

I thought for a short while. I knew what I was about to do was wrong, but I didn't see any other way out. I didn't want to die, and as my wife, it was Braylen's duty to help me. So, with that, I agreed to allow Banks to take Braylen for an entire week.

I watched as Banks placed the chainsaw on the ground next to him. He continued to walk toward me before holding his hand out toward one of his goons. The goon pulled a hunting knife from his pocket and handed it to Banks. Taking the knife from the sheath, he grabbed my index finger before slicing off the tip.

"Ahhhh," I screamed as I watched blood squirt from my finger.

"That's yo reminder not to fuckin' play with me. Now, let's go get yo wife," Banks spoke. "Untie him," he continued, looking over at his goons.

"Wait, we can't just go get her right now. I need some time. She don't know anything about this, so I can't just spring it on her. You have to give me a day or two to talk her into doing it."

Banks nodded his head, understanding what I was saying. Even though Banks was about his business, he wasn't totally heartless, so he would at least give me some time to talk to my wife. With that, Banks agreed that he would wait until Monday to pick her up but would be there first thing that morning. "I'm going to have eyes on you too, so don't try nothing stupid. That won't be good for you."

Blood was everywhere as I looked down at my finger in disbelief. I knew I would need to stop the bleeding and get myself to a hospital quickly. I knew Banks had showed me grace by not killing me, so in my eyes, I was glad it was just the tip of my finger that was missing. As soon as I was untied, I would wrap this finger, and once he dropped me off, I would go to the hospital.

"I promise I won't. I just need to talk to her and let her know what's going on. Monday morning when you come, she'll be ready."

Banks agreed, allowing his goons to place me back into his SUV and take me back home. Banks drove off, smiling hard as hell. I knew he was thinking about the deal we'd just made, and I was happy he was willing to accept Braylen over the hundred thousand I didn't have.

Chapter Three

BRAYLEN

I sat on the couch, looking at the clock every two minutes. It was after nine in the morning, and Kyrie still hadn't returned home. After a night out with Vita, I'd returned home late, only to find that my husband still hadn't returned. As I sat on the couch, waiting for his arrival, my blood boiled. I had no clue where he was or who he was with. Out of all the things Kyrie had put me through, cheating hadn't been a problem since we'd gotten married. However, I wouldn't put it past him either. If he'd done it once, there was nothing stopping him from doing it again.

I sat on the couch, looking out my back patio doors. The sun was shining, and it seemed to be a beautiful day. Yet all I could think about was the fact that my husband had been out all night. A few moments later, I heard the front door open, and I jumped up from the couch, rushing to the door to confront Kyrie.

"Where the hell have you been all fucking night? You think you can let the sun beat yo ass home, and I'm just going to be okay with that shit? Kyrie, you are a fucking married man!" I yelled, letting Kyrie know just how furious I was with him.

I stopped in my tracks when I looked over at my husband and realized he was bloody and beaten. His eye was purple and was swollen to the size of a tennis ball. His lip was busted, and his nose was bloody.

There was so much blood that I couldn't tell where it was all coming from.

"Oh, my God! Kyrie, what happened?"

"I got my ass beat. That's what happened. I need to go to the hospital." Kyrie held up his hand, showing me his half missing finger.

"Oh, my God, Kyrie!"

I rushed off, running up the stairs. When I returned, I had on a pair of sweatpants and my purse was in hand. I slipped into a pair of Crocs before helping Kyrie out to the car, peeling out of the parking lot, and making my way to the hospital. The entire time he'd been out, I'd never thought one time that something could have happened to him. My heart broke as I looked over at his battered face.

When we arrived at the hospital, I parked at the door, and we both rushed in. I could tell he was losing a lot of blood and prayed he would be okay. He was rushed to the back immediately, and I went to park the car. Kyrie didn't have the tip of his missing finger, so they weren't able to reattach it. However, they stitched it up and placed a bandage around it. They also gave him an x-ray and found that he had several broken ribs. When asked what happened to him, Kyrie never spoke a word. Several hours later, we were back in the car and headed home.

"Are you going to at least tell me who did this to you, Kyrie?" I asked as I pulled into the parking lot of our townhome.

"I owe a very bad man a lot of money, and he wants it back. I ended up getting the money but got robbed this morning. Them muthafuckas took everything I had, including the money I was going to pay him back with. As soon as I got back to the house, he was already here and ready for his money. When he realized I didn't have it, he put me in the back of his SUV. I barely got away with my life."

"What? Who do you owe?"

"Banks."

"What the fuck, Kyrie? Why would you borrow money from anybody when you don't have a job to pay it back? Does that make any sense to you? Damn, Kyrie. I got about a thousand dollars. I was saving it for the week to have some fun while I'm on vacation, but you can have that. How much you owe him?"

"A hundred thousand," he replied weakly.

"What the fuck did you just say?" I shifted in my seat, turning to look directly at Kyrie. "You borrowed a hundred thousand American dollars from somebody? Nigga, you have a hundred thousand in cash, and I was at that damn plant working twelve hour shifts every fucking day? Why you over here acting like you can't pay no bills if you got a hundred thousand dollars?"

"I don't have it anymore! That shit been gone."

"Gone? What the fuck you spend the money on, Kyrie? Because from where I sit, it don't look like a hundred thousand worth of nothing is up in here!"

I couldn't believe what I was hearing. *How the fuck did he have all this money and didn't give me one dime of it? He sat here and watched me struggle and did not help at all. He saw how tired I was every night coming home, and he had a pocket full of money? What the fuck kind of man would do something like that to his wife?* I tried to calm down as I took several deep breaths. However, knowing my husband had allowed me to work my fingers to the bone when I didn't have to broke my heart.

"Can you stop talking about that money? That shit is gone and clearly not coming back. I'm trying to tell you how I almost died. That nigga was about to kill me, and I almost didn't get away, and all you thinkin' about is the money?"

I shook my head. It was clear to me that Kyrie was only thinking about himself like he usually did. Turning the car off, I opened the door to get out. I'd heard enough. As I walked up to the front door, I heard Kyrie close behind me. I sighed deeply as I placed my key into the lock and turned the knob. I walked into the living room, placing my purse onto the coffee table before speaking again.

"How did you get away?"

"I promised to give him something."

"What did you promise, Kyrie? Because I don't have a hundred thousand to just jack off like you did."

"You," Kyrie spoke in a low tone. He stared down at the floor when he said it, knowing that I was about to call him everything but a child of God.

"What the fuck did you just say?" I asked, smacking my hand down on my knee. This time, I was yelling. Standing to my feet, I looked down at Kyrie. "What the fuck did you say, Kyrie? Because I know you didn't just say what I think you said. I just know you fucking didn't."

"Braylen, that's the only way I could leave there with my life. He had a chainsaw. You think I want to be cut up into pieces? He already took my finger. What else you think he was gon' do to me? Is that what you want for me? I'm your fucking husband; you would want something like that to happen to me? If you can save my life, why wouldn't you want to?"

"You can't be fucking serious," I scoffed. My heart broke as I looked into Kyrie's eyes and saw the seriousness in them.

"I'm very serious, and he agreed. It was the only thing that would stop him from killing me."

With those words, I stormed off. My eyes burned as tears began to fall from them. I ran up the stairs into the bedroom I shared with my husband. I sat on the bed we'd made love on just two days ago and cried. *How can this be the man I married? He loves me, but he would sell me to another man for a hundred thousand dollars?* My feelings were crushed, and all I could do was cry.

"Baby, why are you crying? It's not even that bad. All you doing is saving the life of your husband. You vowed to do just that, now you want to go back on that shit?" Kyrie asked, walking into the room.

"I also vowed to be only yours, now here you are, trying to sell me like you the pimp and I'm some ho. How is this love? What the fuck is wrong with you, Kyrie?"

Tears fell from my eyes rapidly as I looked to him for an answer. Whatever he said wouldn't matter to me though. There was nothing he could ever say to make this better. I felt worthless as I listened to the man I loved tell me he'd sold me for a debt. On top of that, he didn't even give me any of the money he wanted to use me to pay back. I was waiting for him to tell me this was some type of sick joke, but he never did.

"I'm telling you to go with him, so you not cheating. That don't go against your vows at all. But you promised to do anything for me, right? Then doing this shouldn't be no problem. This one move will save my life, and we will be together forever like you said you wanted to be the day we got married."

"Kyrie, are you listening to yourself?"

"Yeah, but the real question is are you listening to me? You gotta go with him, Bray. It's the only way."

"I need some time to think about this, Kyrie. This is a lot."

"Don't take too much time. He's coming to pick you up first thing Monday morning, and you need to be ready."

I shook my head before watching Kyrie walk out of our room, closing the door behind him. Out of all the things Kyrie could do to me, pimping me out was never supposed to be one of them. My husband, the man that was supposed to love me and protect me, was willingly offering me to another man. I felt like nothing as I curled up into a ball on my bed, crying myself to sleep.

I didn't wake up until almost ten that evening. Walking into the bathroom, I took a hot shower before putting on a black and white cotton nightgown. Walking downstairs, I smelled the food cooking and walked directly into the kitchen.

"Hey there, sleepy head. Dinner is almost ready. Why don't you take a seat at the kitchen table, and I'll bring you a glass of wine?" Kyrie suggested.

Not having the strength to do anymore fighting, I took a seat at the table. Kyrie poured me a glass of red wine before handing it over to me. I sipped from the glass as I watched Kyrie put chicken wings, mashed potatoes, and green beans onto a plate before placing it down on the table in front of me. He'd never cooked anything for me in all the years we'd been together. Now he wanted to pick a time when he only had four fingers on one hand to do so. I hadn't eaten anything all day long and was extremely hungry. The food looked delicious, so I picked up a chicken wing and bit it.

"Is the food good?" Kyrie asked.

"Yeah, it's fine."

"Did you think about going yet? If you don't go, Banks is going to kill me."

"The fact that you want to send me to a man you're scared of yourself is crazy to me. If he would kill you, what do you think he would do to me?"

"He won't hurt you at all. You're a beautiful woman, Braylen; he just needs some eye candy. Maybe some arm candy too. Whatever he does, you don't have to worry about him killing you like he would me. Please, baby, just save my life. It's only for a week. This time next week, you'll be back home with me where you belong, and everything will be good."

Kyrie took a seat at the table across from me, placing his hand on mine before smiling at me. Normally, his smile would win me over; however, this time, I wasn't having it. I snatched my hand away from his and continued to eat my meal.

"Kyrie, the man has already cut off your finger, and you expect me to believe he wouldn't hurt me? And what you mean only a week? A whole fucking week? I thought this was supposed to be an overnight thing, and you agreed to give me to him for an entire week? Kyrie, why would you do that?"

"I need you, Bray. I just need you to be there for me the way a wife should."

I looked at Kyrie. The truth was I was completely disgusted by him, and at this point, I didn't even know if I wanted to be his wife at all. The fact that he would sacrifice me by putting me on the front line was crazy to me. However, anything would be better than spending another day with him, so with that, I agreed.

The next day, I woke up in bed alone. I didn't know where my husband was nor did I care. Getting out of bed, I walked into the bathroom, releasing my bladder. The agony I felt was unlike anything I'd ever experienced. I'd cried all I could cry, and my tears had done nothing. My husband still wanted me to go with a man I didn't know anything about in exchange for money I knew nothing about. *Is this what a good wife would do? Or is this something that a horrible husband has done?* I thought to myself.

Turning on the shower, I stepped inside, allowing the hot water to run down my body. I was numb to everything,, and all I wanted to do was get as far away from Kyrie as I could. If that meant going with a man that I didn't know, then so be it. *Anything gotta be better than being here with Kyrie's ass.*

Once out of the shower, I dried off before putting on a pair of pink sweatpants and a white tank. Walking back into my room, I pulled a suitcase from my closet. I then began going through my closet, piecing together outfits to bring with me. I didn't have many designer pieces, but the few I did have, I was taking with me, including a black Chanel mini dress that I would be putting on Monday morning when Banks arrived to pick me up.

Although I didn't know Banks personally, I knew of him as a big-time hustler in the streets of Detroit. I didn't know what he sold; however, I could only assume it was drugs. Either way, I knew he was a very dangerous yet well-dressed man. If I would be stepping out with him, I would need to look the part, maybe even make Kyrie a bit jealous. I planned to look so good tomorrow morning that Kyrie would think twice about making me go.

"Make sure you pack some of them smell goods you be wearing so that you can smell good around Banks," Kyrie called out, walking into the bedroom.

"I know how to pack my own suitcase, Kyrie. I don't need any help from you. You have done enough."

With that, Kyrie exited the room, leaving me to be able to pack in peace. The rest of the day went by, and I barely said two words to Kyrie. I stayed in our bedroom most of the day, watching TV, while Kyrie stayed in the living room. When I got hungry, I placed an order on Uber Eats, not getting anything for Kyrie. That night when it was time for bed, instead of Kyrie sleeping in our bed next to me, I forced him to sleep on the couch.

That next morning, Kyrie woke me up bright and early. Rolling over to look at the clock, I saw it was only seven in the morning. He didn't know what time Banks would be here to get me, but he wanted to ensure I would be dressed and ready to go when he arrived. Angrily, I got out of bed, walking out the room, and headed to the bathroom. I still had nothing to say to Kyrie, and I could tell he didn't care. The only thing that mattered to him was that I went with Banks so that he would live another day.

I allowed the hot water to run down my body as I lathered my towel with soap, cleansing my body before grabbing my loofah and pouring body wash onto it. Once I was done showering, I stepped out the shower and grabbed a towel before looking at myself in the mirror. My eyes were red and puffy from the crying I'd done the night before. Kyrie knew I didn't want to go, but none of that mattered to him. If I didn't go with him and Banks did kill him, then I wouldn't have to worry about his ass anymore.

However, I knew I couldn't do that. The truth was I truly loved Kyrie, and when I took those vows the day we were married, they were for better or worse. This must be the worse they were talking about. Although I was angry at him, I couldn't see my life without him. There was no way I could allow my husband to be murdered when there was something I could do to stop it.

I oiled my body, being sure to saturate every inch. Once back in my room, I put the towel into the dirty clothes basket that set in the corner of my room before going over to my drawer and pulling out my shapewear. With me not being in the gym lately, I needed something to snatch me in and make me look good in my dress. Walking over to the makeshift vanity, which was really just a small table and chair that I'd hung a mirror above, I plugged up my curlers. I took a seat before taking my hair out of the ponytail it was always in. If I wanted to make Kyrie jealous, I knew I would have to look better than I looked on the daily.

Parting my hair, I began placing curls in it before styling it to the best of my ability. I was no cosmetologist, but my hair turned out good. Once I was done, I applied my makeup, and although it wasn't even nine in the morning, I was starting the day off with a full beat. Red lips and all. Once I was done, I smiled at myself in the mirror, knowing that I should doll myself up more often. I'd just gotten dressed when Kyrie walked into the room. I knew I looked good, but the look on Kyrie's face only confirmed it.

"Damn, you look good. I didn't think you would dress up to go see him. You done did yo hair and everything," Kyrie spoke.

The black mini dress I wore fit me nicely, and the shapewear had my curves on full display. My perky breasts sat up in the low-cut dress, and as I watched Kyrie take a glimpse at my thick thighs, I could see his manhood rise in his pants. I smiled as I grabbed my Bath and Body Works spray and sprayed it all over my body.

"I just want him to get his money's worth. I mean, he did pay for me, right?"

Grabbing my suitcase, I made my way down the stairs. I smiled in the inside with each step I took, knowing that Kyrie was having second thoughts about me going. I knew once he saw me in this dress, he would be eating his words. I heard Kyrie running down the stairs, and I knew this was it. He was about to tell me that I couldn't go. Tell me that he was making a huge mistake and could never send me with another man. I turned around, smiling, waiting for my husband to tell me he'd been moving like a damn fool.

He grabbed my hands, taking them into his, as he looked deeply in my eyes. I knew that seeing me all dressed up to go out with another man would completely change his mine. Knowing that I would soon be unpacking and putting my pajamas back on, I waited for him to speak.

"Since you're going with Banks for the week, you not gon' need that thousand you saved for yo vacation. You should just give it to me since I'm the one that's going to need it to survive through the week."

My mouth dropped open, not believing the words that had just left his lips. My heart broke into pieces as I looked into his eyes, seeing that he was serious. There was no apology for what he had done. Fuck the fact that he'd watched me work hard every day for this money when he had thousands of dollars to just gamble away. There was not an ounce of remorse in his tone as he looked at me, waiting for me to give him my money.

With nothing left, I pulled my phone from my purse and sent a Cash App to Kyrie. I wanted to cry, but I refused to let anymore tears fall. I'd given too many of my tears to Kyrie, and at this point, I had nothing left to give him. There was a knock at the door, and I hoped it was Banks. As scared as I was to spend a week alone with him, I knew that anything would be better than staying here with the man I called my husband.

Kyrie walked over to the door, opening it and allowing a tall, dark-skinned man to walk inside. He stood about six foot four inches tall and had skin so rich it resembled bakers' chocolate. I could tell he stayed in the gym by his muscular frame, while his long locs were neatly twisted into a low ponytail. He smiled at me, showing all thirty-two of his pearly white teeth. He wore a black suit that looked like it was tailor made exclusively for him. He walked into our home, bypassing Kyrie and walking directly to me.

"Good morning, beautiful. I'm Banks, and you will be accompanying me this week. It's very nice to meet you." Banks extended his hand to me, and I shook it.

"It's nice to meet you as well. I'm ready to go when you are. That's my suitcase by the door."

Banks looked down at the large pink suitcase before grabbing it and walking out the door. I took one last look at Kyrie, shaking my head at him. *This muthafucka really not gon' stop me?* Turning around, I walked out the door, not saying another word to Kyrie. There was a man in a black suit standing at the back door of a black SUV. He took my suitcase from Banks before opening the back passenger doors for both of us. After putting the suitcase in the trunk, he got into the driver's seat before pulling off.

I didn't speak much on the ride to Banks' home. I was more upset that I was on my way to his house than anything. I couldn't believe that Kyrie had allowed this to happen. Any fear I had of what Banks might do to me was replaced with anger. In fact, I silently challenged Banks to attempt to hurt me, knowing I would take out every ounce of anger I had for Kyrie on him. I hoped it didn't come to that point, but if it did, I would be prepared.

Forty-five minutes later, we were pulling up to a massive estate. I'd never seen a house so huge and was in awe that I would be staying here for the next week. The house set on so much land that I knew it would take me days before I would be able to see it all. As we drove up the driveway that seemed to be at least a quarter of a mile long, I took notice of the tennis and basketball courts as well as the pool. At the very least, I wouldn't be bored while I was here.

The driver parked in front of the house, getting out of the SUV and opening the door for us. When I got out the car and looked at the house, I stood there for several moments with my mouth open. I'd never seen anything so extravagant, and I smiled at the thought of this being my new residence for the next week. The house was light gray with black trim and a beautiful light gray walkway lined with small black lights that led up to massive steps and a glass front door.

"Do you like the house?" Banks asked, walking over and standing next to me.

"It is beautiful. You live here?"

"Yes, this is my home. I normally don't bring people here, but because this occasion deserves to be celebrated, I felt like sharing my most prized possession with you."

"What's the occasion?" I asked, looking up at Banks.

"You being here with me is the occasion. I promise you this week will be one you will never forget. There are a few rules for the week, which we will get to in a moment. First, I want you to pick out your room and get settled. Before anything, I want you to be comfortable here."

Banks took my hand in his as he led me up the stairs that led to the front door. Walking inside the house, I was taken aback by the grand entryway. The marble flooring and crystal chandeliers were a beautiful introduction to the home, and the floor to ceiling windows gave the home a modern look. I could tell just from walking in that Banks had expensive taste.

"How many bedrooms are in here? This is huge."

"Ten, but there is also a full apartment in the basement with two more bedrooms."

"Damn, I could only aspire to live in a house this big."

"Come on. Let me show you the rest of the house."

Banks walked me around the home, showing me all three stories. We walked inside every room of the home, including the in-house gym as well as the home theater, sauna, and indoor pool. When we got to the last room on the first floor, Banks informed me that it was the door to his office, and it was kept locked because it was off limits. He let me know that I had free reign of the house and could go anywhere on the estate except for his office. I happily agreed, already pleased with what I'd seen. However, I couldn't help but wonder what Banks was hiding in there.

"You can choose to stay in any of the rooms that you want to. You can also choose to stay in the master bedroom with me if you like," Banks suggested.

I smiled, respectfully declining staying in the master suite with Banks. Instead, I chose a room on the second floor of the home. It was decorated in cream, taupe, and chocolate tones which gave the room a warm and cozy feel. The king-sized bed set on a platform that you had to walk up two steps to get to. There was also an en-suite bathroom equipped with a claw foot tub and a separate rain shower.

"I left my suitcase in your truck. I gotta go down and get it."

"It's no need. I can have someone bring it to your room. But you won't be wearing anything in that suitcase while you're here with me."

"What do you mean?" I asked, confused.

"Just as I said, nothing you brought with you will be worn inside my home. Other men have seen you in it before I have. More importantly, yo so called husband has seen you in that shit before I have. I'll have Sabrina show you several pieces and allow you to choose whatever you want."

"Who is Sabrina?" I asked, even more confused.

"She's my stylist, and she will take good care of you."

I nodded my head before Banks led me down to the kitchen. The entire kitchen was black and white. There were black marble counter-tops and an island in the middle. There were also black appliances and a black dining table with matching black leather chairs. White roses in a white vase set in the middle of the table while black and white abstract paintings adorned the white walls. There was a chef standing at the stove, preparing a breakfast of eggs benedict, hash browns, and fresh fruit.

Banks pulled out my chair, and I took my seat before he did the same. The chef made our plates before serving us at the table. It was the most elegant scene, and if this was the treatment I would be receiving for the week, then I was going to enjoy being here. Kyrie thought he was ruining my vacation, doing this shit, when really, he did me a damn favor. I was going to make the best of this and live like a queen doing it. We ate in silence for several moments before Banks began running down the rules of my stay.

"I've already given you two of my main rules; however, there are a few more. Rule one, there will be no contact with your husband for the next week. No phone calls, no texts, no meet ups, none of that shit. You are mine for the week, so you won't be entertaining any other men."

Shit, I don't want to talk to that nigga at all, so you don't even have to worry about that, I thought to myself. I didn't have a damn thing to say to Kyrie and felt I needed to reevaluate him being in my life at all. Nodding my head, I agreed with Banks' rule before he moved on to the next.

"Lastly, we need to come up with a safe word when it comes to sex. I expect you to try everything that may happen over this next week; however, if anything gets to be too much for you, then we need to have a safe word that you can use, so I know not to take things further."

"A safe word for sex?" I asked, confused.

"Yes, things are gon' get wild as fuck around here, so I'd suggest we create one. If you don't want to, that's on you, but the word stop is not in my vocabulary when it comes to sex."

I looked at Banks for a moment, and seriousness was etched all over his face. What the fuck kind of sex needed a damn safe word? I'd never been asked this before. I'd only had one other boyfriend besides Kyrie, and neither of them needed a safe word when it came to sex. However, the fact that he wanted to create one further intrigued me. *What kind of freaky ass shit did Kyrie get me into?*

"Um, I've never been asked this before." I laughed shyly, covering my mouth. "Why would we need a safe word?"

Although I'd only had two sexual partners in my life, I still considered myself well-seasoned when it came to sex. My first boyfriend taught me a lot about pleasing a man, so Kyrie never had any complaints. I was sure that I could hang with Banks when it came to sex seeing how Kyrie could go for hours.

"Braylen, I'm sure you don't understand what this week means. For this week, your body is mine, every part of you. You will be mine to do as I see fit, and that means nothing is off limits. I will be utilizing every part of your body, and some things will be foreign to you, I'm sure. I want you to feel comfortable however, so if at any point things become more than you can handle, we need a safe word so that I know to ease up a bit."

I saw the seriousness in his deep brown eyes as I looked at him. I thought for a minute, trying to come up with a safe word to give to Banks. After several moments of coming up with nothing, I thought about things I liked to do. Thinking of my favorite drink, I smiled before opening my mouth to speak.

"Hennessy. The safe word is Hennessy."

"I like that. That's my favorite drink."

"Mine too." I smiled.

"Okay, then Hennessy is the safe word. Use it when you need to but use it wisely because you can only use it once a day. Once you have already used the word, you can't use it again until the next day."

"Okay, I'll keep that in mind."

When we were both done eating, Banks pulled out his phone, placing a call before putting the phone on speaker. I listened as a female answered the phone, and Banks told her he needed her at his house within the hour. She agreed with no hesitation before ending the call.

Chapter Four

BANKS

Sabrina arrived about forty-five minutes later. When I opened the door, she let me know that she had several items in her car that needed to be brought in. Shooting a text to my driver, Zeek, I let him know to have everything brought up to Braylen's room before walking Sabrina into the kitchen to meet Braylen. They hit it off instantly with Sabrina letting Braylen know she had several pieces she knew she would love. I let Sabrina know which room was Braylen's, and the two of them disappeared upstairs. Knowing they would be occupied for at least a few hours, I decided to make my way to the home office. Although I'd planned on taking the entire week off while Braylen was here, due to unforeseen circumstances, that now wouldn't be possible.

The sound of the door clicking shut behind me echoed throughout the air as I stepped into my office. The silence was not the sound of peace but the sound of fear, the dreadful silence you heard right before the worst thing in your life happened. Every time I stepped into my office and the door clicked behind me, I knew someone in the world was about to experience that silence. However, for me, it was the sound of total control. I loved my house; however, this one room was my sanctuary.

The room wasn't massive; it was actually the smallest bedroom in my house that I had converted into my home office. However, it had everything I needed to do my job in one room, and those were the details that mattered. Size never equaled power. The dark cherrywood floor was rich and smooth beneath the soles of my custom Ferragamo loafers. The walls were matte black obsidian that didn't reflect light but instead sucked it in. The ceiling was coffered and trimmed in gunmetal gray. That was how I liked it, deep and dark with no outside light.

To the right was a floor-to-ceiling bookshelf that stretched across the entire wall. However, there were no paperbacks on my bookshelf. You would never find any fiction, fantasy, or none of those freak nasty books that were popular here. My bookshelf housed different types of books. Each shelf was lined with black leather binders, numbered in gold and placed neatly on the shelves. Inside the binders were records, transactions, names, and prices. There were a few royal blue folders locked behind smoked glass.

On the left wall was a mounted display case which ran the length of the wall. It housed my weapons, some old, some new. There were curved daggers, several pairs of brass knuckles, a blade I took off a man who thought he could rob me out in Inkster, and over two dozen guns. It was my playground, my fun land, my Six Flags Over Detroit. I could take down an entire army with this one display case alone.

The windows stretched tall on the wall directly in front of me, taking up the entire wall behind my desk. They were floor-to-ceiling and had triple-paned glass with motorized blackout shades half drawn. My outdoor pool was the view with the beautiful green trees behind it. My desk was the centerpiece, a custom-made, black, glass desk. It was heavy, solid like me. It set atop a black Persian rug. On top of my desk set a crystal decanter filled with cognac that cost more than most people's rent. There was also a matte black laptop encrypted with codes only I would know. Beside my laptop, there was a .45 caliber pistol, polished and ready for whoever.

Taking off my Armani suit jacket, I draped it across my chair before taking a seat. I sank into the soft leather, Italian and black like everything else inside my office. I reached into my cigar case and grabbed a cigar. It was Cuban, the real kind. Clipping the tip, I lit it with a gold butane torch and inhaled. Smoke curled around me as the scent of tobacco mixed with the faint smell of saffron. I clicked on my playlist, and Tupac played through the built-in speakers.

Opening my laptop, I powered it on and waited for it to boot up. Most people talked about power like it was supposed to be loud and flashy. To them, power came in the form of chains, cars, and stacks of money they tossed around on TikTok or Instagram. However, that shit wasn't power. A nigga with real power like me knew that real power whispered, not roared. The moment my laptop booted up, I instantly saw a new request in my secured inbox. Opening the tab, I read the message. The client, a private contractor. Their request, a female, age range twenty to twenty-five who must be multilingual. My payment, one point two million in the form of a wire transfer that would be initiated upon delivery.

My eyes scanned the email, reading over it twice, being sure I had all the details correct. I didn't sell drugs like some people may have thought. That shit was for the amateurs. Selling drugs was too messy, too exposed. The Feds had been cracking down on the drug game since the eighties, so that wasn't my speed at all. I didn't move product; I moved people. It was not like them sloppy ass traffickers they showed on TV. I didn't run bitches out of trap houses or filthy motel rooms. I wasn't chaining no ho to a radiator in some nasty ass abandoned building. What I did was high-end, next level shit that regular people couldn't even touch.

I dealt in requests only. People came to me when they wanted specifics, something rare, something no one else could find. When you came to me, you were sure, and you had the money to back it up. My roster was encrypted and categorized and could only be accessed with a biometric scan. Dozens of faces popped up on screen of all races. Each face had a file attached to it, allowing me to know everything I needed to know. I scrolled until I found her, alias Sunflower 25. A twenty-two-year-old Black college student that spoke English, French, and Arabic. She'd been lured in through a fake talent agency site that was ran by one of my Florida recruiters.

I smiled, knowing that she was a perfect match for what was asked for. I selected her file and pasted it into the folder marked for the contractor. Instantly, an alert chimed, letting me know that a van would arrive in six hours to transport her to the designated area. Soon, she would be in transit. Within seventy-two hours, she'd be out of the country, and I would be over a million dollars richer. I took another pull from my cigar and smiled.

What I did wasn't easy, and if you had morals, it would be next to impossible. However, for me, it was business as usual. People didn't understand. They thought they did, but they didn't. They thought evil wore a ski mask and crept through the night, waiting to catch you slipping. That wasn't the case though. Evil didn't hide in alleyways or slip into your house at night. Real evil wore suits and sipped expensive cognac. Real evil sat behind desks, drove foreign cars, and lived in gated communities. I was evil, and I was okay with that. It was a job, and someone had to do it.

There was another email marked important. I double clicked it, opening it before reading the contents. It was short and straight to the point. Alias Watermelon 34 escaped. My jaws clenched, and I poured a shot of cognac into a glass before placing it to my lips, allowing the liquor to run down my throat. Sending a reply back, I had questions. When did she escape and how? My warehouses were guarded to the tee for this reason alone. No one should be able to escape, and if someone did, that meant my men were not doing their jobs. They would have to pay for that. However, first, they would have to find the girl.

Leaning back in my chair, I took a pull from my cigar then exhaled. I was done working for the day. Anything else that needed my attention would have to wait until tomorrow. Walking up to Braylen's room, I was just about to walk in when the door opened, and Sabrina jumped back.

"Shit, you scared me. I didn't even hear you knock."

"That's because I didn't."

Walking into the room, I saw Braylen standing in a black, Marine Serre, bodycon dress that showed off her thick thighs. She smiled when she looked over at me. I looked into her beautiful brown eyes, and I almost felt bad for her. Here she was, a beautiful woman who was only here because the man she chose to marry offered her up as collateral. As fucked up as it was, I was still going to get my money's worth.

"I got her together for you, Banks. She picked out a daytime and an evening look for every day she would be here with shoes and bags to match. I also threw in a few bathing suits just in case she wanted to go swimming while she was here. I can show myself out, and you can just have everything she didn't choose boxed up, and I'll get it the next time I'm here. Sorry to rush outta here, but I have another client to get to in twenty minutes, and I don't want to be late."

"No problem. Thank you for coming. I'll be sure to add a little extra to the invoice for the short notice."

Sabrina smiled, thanking me, before walking out the room.

"This was so sweet of you, Banks. I love everything. Thank you."

"Now, we need to go to Neiman's and get yo ass some real perfume. You can't be smelling like that cheap ass body mist when you with me. Put the shoes on you got to match that dress, grab the purse, and let's go."

I walked out the room before she could even answer. This wasn't a question. This was an order. Kyrie may have allowed her to walk around, looking and smelling cheap, but that shit wasn't going to fly with me. If Braylen was going to be a reflection of me, even if it was just for a week, she was going to look the part. Sliding my phone from my pocket, I called Zeek and asked him to pull the car around. Several moments later, Braylen walked down the stairs.

"You know, you don't have to be so rude. If you didn't like the fragrance I was wearing, you could have just said that. Calling it cheap was uncalled for."

I walked over to her, getting close to her, so that she would fully understand what I was about to say. There was no need to raise my voice because I knew she would understand exactly what I was saying. So, in a low tone, I replied. "You don't challenge me – ever. If I say something, that's what it is. I'm sorry if we got off on the wrong foot, and you thought your opinion mattered, but it doesn't. If you think I'm rude, keep that shit to yoself because trust me when I tell you you ain't seen rude. The last thing you want to do is disobey what I'm telling you. That wouldn't be good for you."

The fear in her eyes let me know she understood what I'd said. With that, I turned around and walked out the door. Braylen didn't say another word, just meekly followed behind me as I made my way out to my SUV. Zeek was already standing there with the back passenger doors open, and we both got inside before he closed them and got into the driver's seat. I rolled down the partition, letting him know we needed to go to Neiman's. Braylen didn't speak to me the entire ride, and that was okay. This was only the first day, and I knew the situation alone would take some time to get used to.

I just hated the way she smelled. It was not because she smelled bad. She didn't stink, but she smelled basic, just like every other bitch that picked up a mist from Bath and Body Works or some roll on oils from the beauty supply store and thought they were doing something. I didn't need a bitch around me smelling like vanilla and desperation.

We walked through the doors of Neiman Marcus and were instantly greeted with the fake smiles of employees wanting to make a sale. They were like vultures that could smell the credit cards through my Italian leather wallet. Braylen walked beside me, still bitter. I knew she wasn't used to this, but this would be her life for the next week.

I stopped in front of the Tom Ford display and turned to her slowly. "Let's start here and work our way through. All the bubblegum and cotton candy shit is out the window. You mine now, so you gon' smell how I want you to smell."

The sales associate made her way to us, her heels clicking against the floor with every step. She greeted us with yet another fake smile. "Can I help the two of you find anything today?"

I pointed to the Tom Ford bottles. "I want her to try Lost Cherry and Fucking Fabulous."

"Fucking Fabulous? What kind of name is that for a perfume?" Braylen laughed.

The sales associate walked up to the display without question and pulled the two bottles down, spraying them on a tester strip before handing them over to Braylen. Her eyes widened as she inhaled each scent. She then placed them up to my nose for me to smell. This was what I needed her to smell like while she was with me, grown and sexy.

"I like those." I nodded. "Can we get both of these in the biggest size?" I turned to the associate.

"Absolutely, I'll be right back."

Braylen walked over to another display. Looking up at the name, I saw it was Versace. She picked up a light pink bottle in the shape of some type of crystal. "What about this one? It's Bright Crystal. I been hearing a lot about this on TikTok."

"No."

"But you haven't even..."

"I said no." I cut her off mid-sentence.

She silenced, remembering what I'd said before we'd left the house. She swallowed hard, returning the bottle to the display before backing away. An old white man looked over at me, turning up his nose while shaking his head. I looked over at him, staring him down, waiting on him to open his mouth. He must have liked life because just as soon as he looked up, he looked away. I stepped closer to Braylen, opting to not make a scene inside the store.

"Don't pick no shit like that up again. If you had good taste in perfume, we wouldn't even be here."

She blinked rapidly, eyes looking up at me. I could tell she wanted to clap back, but the fear inside her prevented that. She nodded her head slowly, letting me know that she understood. I walked over to another display – Maison Francis Kurkdjian. Picking up two bottles, Baccarat Rouge 540 and Gentle Fluidity Gold, I sprayed them both onto a tester. I placed them up to her nose one by one for her to smell.

"This smells like a woman that knows her worth and won't settle for less. You might learn a lot from smelling like this."

She looked up at me again, like she couldn't believe what I'd just said. She bit her bottom lip in an effort to stop it from trembling. I looked deep into her eyes, silently challenging her to crash out. I knew my slick remarks were getting to her, but I didn't give a fuck. She didn't know her worth. That was clear due to the circumstances behind her even being with me. So, I would treat her the way she treated herself until she showed me otherwise.

When the sales associate walked back over to us with the bottles I'd requested, I showed her the final two bottles, letting her know I wanted them in a bigger size as well. She smiled before turning right back around. Arriving a few moments later with those bottles, I told her to bag everything and walked up to the counter to pay. I grabbed the bag before Braylen and I walked back out to my SUV.

"I didn't think my perfume smelled that bad. I kinda like the scent," she announced once we were inside the car and had pulled out the parking lot.

"Please. You takin' a shower as soon as we get back to the house. That shit smells like a damn high school hallway."

Braylen frowned before she burst out into laughter. "Dawg, a high school hallway, really? Come on now. That shit wasn't that bad."

"Yeah, okay." I cracked a half smile.

When we arrived back to my house, Braylen wasted no time doing what I'd ordered and went directly up to her room to shower. I told her to choose any one of the perfumes I'd just bought her and put it on. She agreed, and I went into my room to shower and get more comfortable.

Chapter Five

BRAYLEN

I couldn't believe the way Banks had just done a one eighty and completely changed. I didn't like the way he was talking to me, and if this was how the week was going to be, I couldn't wait for it to be over. I stood in the shower, washing every part of my body, being sure to wash the Bath and Body Works from my body. Once out the shower, I dried off before taking the shea butter that set on the bathroom counter and rubbing it all over my body. Then, I made my way out to the bedroom area and sprayed my body with Tom Ford's Lost Cherry.

I couldn't lie; I liked the scent. It was much better than any cherry scent I'd ever smelled. Before I could pick out the next outfit for me to put on, I heard my door open. Jumping back, I covered myself as I saw Banks walk inside the room. There was no knock. He simply walked inside and up to me, grabbing me before deeply inhaling my scent.

"Now you smell like a grown woman," he spoke.

His arm was wrapped around me tightly, and I flinched in fear. His touch was foreign to my bare skin. He wore a pair of gray sweatpants that showed the print of his thick manhood which hung down his thigh. His locs hung down his back, and he smelled so good. I knew it was something expensive. The heat formed between my thighs, and I knew my body was about to betray me. I didn't appreciate the way

Banks had spoken to me today. I was pissed at him. But I was even more so pissed at the fact that I was standing there, getting wet for this man.

"What are you doing?" I whispered.

He didn't answer. Instead, he walked across the room and took a seat on the bed. Still not saying a word, he motioned for me to come to him. I could feel the order in the motion, and I didn't protest. Slowly, I walked over to him, standing in front of him as he eyed my body. He looked me up and down as if he was scanning for imperfections. I knew he didn't like my body. He couldn't. I might have looked good in clothes. However, naked, he could see every bit of lose skin and fat rolls I had.

Reaching up, he gently ran his fingers over my thigh. Goosebumps formed over my entire body, and my nipples hardened. My body shook from both nervousness and his touch. I wanted him to stop and keep going all at the same time.

"Come here."

I was already standing in front of him. If I got any closer, I would be on top of him. Maybe that was what he wanted. I looked in his eyes deeply before slightly bending over. He grabbed the back of my neck, pulling me into him. He kissed me. However, the kiss wasn't as gentle as his touch. It wasn't sweet or welcoming. Instead, it was controlling, almost as if he dared me to reject him. Grabbing my hair, he pushed me back just enough for him to speak.

"You remember the safe word?"

"Yes," I managed, breath caught somewhere between passion and lust.

I didn't understand how I wanted this man so badly. He was just going the fuck off on me inside a store and basically told me I stank. Yet here I was, longing to feel him inside of me. My eyes traced the ink all over his neck, chest, ribs, and arms. He was solid and strong, and I licked my lips as I eyed him. His muscles flexed with his every move.

"Lay down," he ordered.

I did as I was told. Climbing onto the bed, crawling to the middle, before lying flat on my back. Banks climbed onto the bed, parting my legs like he owned them. His fingers trailed up my thigh. Before I knew it, he slid two fingers inside of me. Arching my back, I moaned out in pleasure.

"You so wet," he whispered, listening to the gushy sounds my pussy made every time he moved his fingers in and out of me. "This shit wet for me already, huh?"

Before I could answer, Banks opened his mouth and replaced his fingers with his tongue. I bit my bottom lip as his mouth devoured me. Kyrie ate my pussy all the time, but it never felt like this. I gripped the sheets as my body trembled. I could feel my orgasm nearing, and the moment he placed his lips around my love button and sucked gently, there it was – the hardest orgasm I'd experienced in my life.

Without giving me time to catch my breath, Banks climbed on top of me, positioning himself between my legs. I hadn't even noticed that he'd already taken off his pants. I tensed, knowing that his thick manhood would be entering me soon. I knew his thickness was about to stretch me to capacity. I was used to Kyrie's dick, and with me not having much to compare it to, it was good. However, the third leg Banks came with scared me. He placed his meaty mushroomed shaped head at my opening before pushing himself into me.

I screamed out in pain as he rammed inside me. However, my screams quickly turned to moans of pleasure as my walls opened for him. He kissed my neck softly before biting down hard on my shoulder blade. I knew it was going to leave a mark, and I was sure those were his intentions. He was staking his claim on my body and marking his territory.

Without warning, he flipped me over and pulled me up on all fours. Using one of his hands, he slapped my ass cheek hard, causing me to yelp. The entire right side of my ass was stinging. Reaching around, he used two fingers to massage my clit, and I moaned deeply. My body was in ecstasy, and I bit my bottom lip when Banks placed his lips to my ear.

"I'm gon' make it so you can't never give this pussy away to nobody else. This tight muthafucka mine now."

I didn't protest. It didn't matter that I was a married woman with another man telling me I now belonged to him. Instead, I arched my back, he grabbed my hips, and I allowed him to have his way with me. Maybe a part of me wanted to be his. Banks was so dark and mysterious, and I wanted more. I needed more. I could tell there were layers to Banks, and he made me want to peel them back one by one. There was no way this man was fucking me this good.

Placing one hand on the small of my back, he pushed down, causing my arch to deepen. I thought he was going to fold me in half. My ass was high in the air as he pumped in and out of me forcefully. I gripped the sheets with both hands, biting the pillow as I took in every inch of him. This had to be what it meant to get your back blown out. We had sex for what seemed like hours, and when we were done, Banks got up and walked out the room without a word.

I laid there, legs still spread, breaths still heavy. My heart pounded, and my juices still flowed from between my thighs. My love box was tender from the damage Banks had just done. Rolling over to my side, I covered myself with the sheet. I felt confused, caught up in lust and wanting more. Was I wrong for wanting him to stay? Why did he just leave like that? Was I the only one that felt the sparks between us? I laid in bed thinking about what had just taken place until I fell asleep.

***

I rolled over the next morning and looked at the clock. It was six in the morning. Pulling the covers back, I got out of bed and walked to the en-suite bathroom. I used the bathroom with last night still heavy on my mind. When I was done using the bathroom, I turned on the shower before stepping inside. The hot water ran down my body as I lathered the loofah with the coconut scented body wash that was already inside the bathroom. I washed my body from head to toe, smiling as I thought about Banks.

Rubbing the loofah over my breasts, my body tingled when I brushed over my nipples. Licking my lips, I used my free hand and twirled one nipple between my thumb and index finger. I moaned softly, allowing the loofah to fall to the shower floor, before inserting two fingers inside me. I moaned as I moved my fingers in and out of me as I closed my eyes. Thoughts of Banks flashed through my mind. My knees began to buckle at both the sensation and the memory of the way his skin felt pressed against mine.

My fingers moved in slow circles as the image of Banks' head between my thighs took over. His voice was deep and dangerous, and I could still hear the words he spoke into my ear. *"I'm gon' make it so you can't never give this pussy away to nobody else."* Just the words alone sent me into another orgasm right there in the shower.

When I was finally done showering, I dried off before again rubbing shea butter all over my body. Walking back into the bedroom area, I looked through the clothes I'd gotten from Sabrina, trying to find some loungewear. When I realized I hadn't picked out any, I opened the suitcase I'd brought with me and found a pair of peach-colored biker shorts with a matching tank top. It was one of the sets I used to workout in but now wore around the house. I sprayed myself with Gentle Fluidity Gold, knowing that Banks would love the way I smelled. I'd just finished brushing my hair into a ponytail when my phone rang. Looking down to see it was Vita, I answered it.

"Girl, where the fuck you at, and why does Kyrie look all fucked up and shit? Nigga walking around with his hand wrapped up and two black eyes. Let me find out you finally knocked his ass between the stove and the refrigerator."

"It's a long story."

"Well, tell that shit. I ain't got nothing but time. Where you at anyway? I came to take you to breakfast, and yo ass ain't even here."

I didn't know what to tell Vita. There was no way I could tell her that I was at a man's house that Kyrie sold me to for a debt he had. There was also no way I could lie to her. She would know the moment I opened my mouth that it was a lie. Before I could say anything, my phone clicked, letting me know I had another call coming through. Taking the phone from my ear, I looked down to see Kyrie's face dancing across my screen. My heart dropped to my stomach knowing I couldn't answer. Banks had made it clear that I was not to talk to Kyrie while I was here with him. Not knowing what else to do, I told Vita I would call her back and ended the call without waiting for her to respond.

Placing my phone inside the nightstand drawer, I walked out the room and headed down to the kitchen. After what Banks gave me last night, I knew that nigga deserved breakfast. I knew he had a personal chef, but I wanted to cook this meal for him myself – sort of a thank you for giving me the dick I'd been missing for the last twenty-five years of my life. The house was quiet, and I knew Banks wasn't awake yet, which was a good thing because I wanted to surprise him.

I walked into the kitchen and opened the fridge, pulling out everything I needed to make omelets. Normally when I cooked, I liked to
listen to music. However, since it wasn't even eight in the morning, I
knew I would have to cook in silence. I washed off red and green bell
peppers and onions before dicing them up. I placed them into a pan
with ground sausage and fired it up. Once it was done, I began cracking
eggs into a bowl, seasoned them, and then began making our omelets. I
placed two pieces of wheat bread into the toaster and began cutting up
fruit. Once everything was ready, I placed it onto our plates. I'd just
finished when Banks walked into the kitchen. He must have smelled the
aroma of the food because he walked in smiling when he noticed I was
the one at the stove.

"You made breakfast?" Banks asked, voice rough from lack of sleep.
There was a hint of surprise in his tone that I almost mistook for
softness.

"I thought you would be hungry after last night, so I decided to
surprise you."

I glanced up at him. Banks looked good shirtless, tattoos covering
his body like pages of a well written book. His locs hung down over his
shoulders as he walked closer to me. He looked at me, and for a second, I
wondered if he wanted a repeat of last night. However, when his gaze
dropped, I knew Banks wasn't pleased about something.

"Where did you get those clothes from? Did Sabrina bring that with
her?" His tone was still low; however, I could feel the firmness.

I blinked. "Um, I brought them with me."

"What did I tell you the rules were in my house?"

My heartbeat quickened. "They're just clothes, Banks. Sabrina
didn't bring any loungewear with her. I didn't want to cook breakfast in
a full designer outfit."

"No, they're not just clothes!" he snapped, causing me to jump. "It
is exactly what I told you not to do!"

"But I didn't have anything else to wear."

"Then you could have went naked. Now, take that shit off!"

"W-what?" I asked, spatula still trembling in my hand.

"Take that shit the fuck off right now. Don't make me say it again."

My eyes filled with tears as I placed the spatula onto the counter and
slid my crop top over my head. I threw it onto the floor before sliding

out of my shorts. I never broke eye contact with Banks as he looked on in approval. I couldn't believe he was acting like this over some damn clothes. I looked up at him, completely naked.

"Are you happy now?" I asked.

Without another word, Banks stormed out of the kitchen, and I stood there, both exposed and confused. I knew he told me that he didn't want me wearing anything I brought with me, but I didn't see the problem with me wearing some around the house clothes when all I was doing was cooking around the house. It was like Banks had a problem with everything I did. Before I could even walk back up to my room, Banks returned to the kitchen, this time with my suitcase. I looked up at him with wide eyes. He wanted me to leave. Hell, by the way he'd acted toward me while I was here, I didn't think leaving was such a bad idea. What would happen to Kyrie if I left before the week was over? Would Banks kill him because I wasn't able to fulfill the agreement?

Before I could ask any of the questions I had, Banks grabbed the clothes he'd just forced me to take off before storming out the door and walking into the backyard. I went to follow him but quickly remembered I was naked. Running up to my room, I pulled out a black Dior mini dress that I'd gotten from Sabrina and put it on. I rushed back down the stairs, running into the kitchen and out the back door. I ran across the lawn, but by the time I'd gotten to Banks, it was too late. Everything I brought with me, which was half of what I owned, had been thrown into his firepit and set ablaze.

I stood there for several seconds with my mouth wide open. Was this nigga serious? Did he really set all my clothes on fire? I went to speak, but before I could, Banks turned to me, eyes filled with rage.

"I don't want to hear shit. I told you I didn't want you wearing any of that shit, and you did it anyway. Your shit is gone because you didn't listen. Now I see why you ended up marrying a nigga like Kyrie. I'm sure a bunch of muthafuckas told you not to do it, but yo ass didn't listen. Come the fuck on so we can eat breakfast and go."

Before I could say anything, Banks walked away, heading across the grass and into the house. I was stunned and didn't know what to do or say. I looked over at my clothes that were quickly turning to ashes before looking back at the house. I knew I wouldn't be able to save my clothes from the burning fire, so instead, I walked back into the house, pissed.

Banks was already sitting at the table with his plate in front of him. My plate was at the table as well, waiting on me. I looked over at Banks, and he smiled at me. He knew I was pissed, but I could tell by the smile he gave me that he didn't care. He motioned for me to take a seat at the table. Although I no longer wanted to have breakfast with him, I took a seat anyway. We ate breakfast in silence, and when Banks was finished, he washed his dish before telling me we would be leaving in thirty minutes.

I had no clue where we were going, and I really didn't give a fuck. This was only my second day here, and I was already sick of Banks. Did he fuck the shit out of me? Yes. However, that didn't make up for the asshole that he was. Deciding to take off the dress, I put on a pair of Bottega jeans I knew cost more than my rent for three months and a white crop top. Keeping up with the Bottega theme, I placed my feet into a pair of nude slides before grabbing a Bottega purse in the same color. I put on a pair of gold hoop earrings and placed some lip gloss on my lips before walking out the room.

I made my way down the stairs to see Banks waiting for me in the foyer. His head was down as he scrolled through his phone. He looked up at me once I made it to the bottom step. He wore a black Amiri t-shirt that looked as though it was made just for him. The Balmain joggers he wore left a nice print of his third leg, while his off-white Nike Air Ones were crisp like they'd never been worn. A plain gold Rolex adorned his wrist, and his locs were in a man bun that rested on the top of his head. I looked at him, hating the fact that my body was betraying me yet again as my juices began to flow between my thighs. I walked closer to him, inhaling the scent of his cologne.

"You smell good. What are you wearing?"

"Oud Wood by Tom Ford." He smirked.

Zeek walked in, letting us know he'd arrived, and the car was out front. Banks motioned for me to come, and we walked out the door.

"Where are we going?" I asked the moment we got into the back of his SUV.

"Target."

"Target?" I questioned in confusion.

"You need some shit to wear around the house, right? Well, that's what we going to get. You need panties and bras too, so we can stop by Pink or something."

With that, we made our way to Target, and Banks replaced everything he'd burned. I was still upset with him because I felt that burning my clothes was a bit extreme; however, I was happy he replaced everything and added extra.

KYRIE

I called Braylen for the fifth time, and she had yet to answer. I knew she was upset with me, but to just not answer my calls was crazy. Deciding I would give it a couple hours before calling her again, I placed a call to Jason. I needed to see if he'd gone to the pawn shop and gotten rid of any of the stolen goods. He let me know he was just leaving the pawn shop and was on his way to my house. The joyful tone in his voice let me know that we'd come out good. Rubbing my hands together, I smiled, ready to see the money we'd made.

Jason arrived about fifteen minutes later, and I led him to the living room. He sat on the couch before pulling two wads of money from his pockets, slapping them down onto the coffee table.

"Ten bands, muthafucka. That's five apiece." He smiled.

"That's it?" I stared at him. There was no way all that jewelry we stole was only worth ten racks.

Jason looked up at me in confusion as his smile quickly turned straight faced. "What you mean that's it? Did you hear me say it was ten bands right here? Ten bands that your ass didn't have yesterday. You was just telling me the other day how Banks was going to kill you if you didn't get him his money. Now you done paid him back and got another five thousand dollars. But somehow you still over here mad.

Nigga, we up. We made all this money, and the lick took less than ten minutes. What the fuck is up with you?"

"Nigga, it took yo ass days to get this shit off, and when you finally do, you come in here with a punk ass ten bands, and you asking what's wrong with me? Nigga, what's wrong with you? I saw the shit we took. That had to be like a hundred racks worth of shit, if not more, and you let it all go for ten? Yo ass got played, and you wanna know what's wrong with me."

I rubbed my hand through my matted braids before taking a seat in one of the yellow accent chairs across from the couch. I couldn't believe how stupid Jason had been. To him, five thousand dollars was a lot of money, but that wasn't shit compared to the other ninety-five thousand more that I needed.

"I don't see why you so mad. We made some good money," Jason continued.

"I need a hundred bands, Jay. That five thousand ain't shit."

"I thought you told me the other day you was straight with that Banks situation?"

I blew out a long breath before looking up at him. "He accepted Braylen instead of the money."

"Nigga, what?"

I held up my wrapped hand. "That nigga was gon' kill me, so I didn't know what else to do. Now, she not answering none of my calls or texts, and all I want to do is talk to her."

"Wait a damn minute. You tellin' me that you got a hundred bands that you couldn't pay back. The nigga found you, clearly beat yo ass, and yo solution was to give him yo wife? Nigga, what the fuck?"

"I don't need a play by play. What I need is to get my wife back."

"Nigga, you sent yo wife to Banks. You better hope you have a wife that will even come back. Everybody in the state know that nigga got money over money, and yo broke ass sent yo wife to be with him? And for how long?"

"A week."

My tone was low because when I said the words out loud, I knew I was wrong. What if Jason was right, and Braylen never came back to me? Shit, the longer she was with Banks, the better the chances of that happening were. I needed to get that money and fast. If I had the money, I could give it to Banks, and I could get Braylen back. I knew that was my only hope. The problem was, I didn't know how I was going to get the money.

"A week? Nigga, you trippin'. I'm trying to figure out how you done sold yo wife to a rich ass nigga, yet I'm the one that's separated." Jason began to laugh but stopped when I looked up at him, letting him know wasn't shit funny. "Okay, my bad, nigga. I'm just saying. But on some real shit, what if we hit up a few more houses? This five thousand came quick, and that was just from one house. What if we hit up a few houses? Shit, we can go right back out to West Bloomfield and have that shit in no time."

"Nigga, is you crazy? Ain't nobody tryna break into houses for a living. That shit gon' have me locked up before I can even get my wife back. I'm good. I'll just figure this shit out on my own."

Jason stayed at my house for about twenty more minutes before leaving.

I called Braylen back a few more times, and just like all the rest, the calls went unanswered. I shot her a text, letting her know that I missed her and wanted to hear her voice, before walking upstairs to the bathroom. I took a shower and got dressed, ready to start my day. I knew I had to get on my shit if I was actually going to get this hundred bands and get my baby back. I had six thousand dollars to my name. Five of them were stacked in crisp bills on my coffee table. I knew I couldn't allow her to stay with him any longer. I thought I could handle it. I thought everything would be good. Yet here I was, going crazy without her.

Braylen was my wife. She was my anchor, and after just one night without her, I was already drowning. I needed her back fast, and I was going to do everything I needed to do to make that happen.

Rushing back down the stairs, I made my way out the door. The sun was shining bright, and it seemed to be a beautiful day. However, there was nothing beautiful about what was happening in my life. Getting into the driver's seat of Braylen's car, I made my way downtown.

I walked inside the room, and instantly the smell of cigarettes and cheap perfume hit my nose. Not wanting to go back to Motor City Casino after being robbed, I decided to go to Greektown. Although this wasn't my usual casino, I hoped I would have some beginner's luck and win some money.

I left the thousand Braylen had given me and only played the five thousand. If I lost this, I would still need some money to make something else shake. Finding the Blackjack table, my game of choice, I took a seat. The pale faced dealer was young with black, spiked hair and a thin lined goatee. I placed the five thousand dollars onto the table, and he slid my chips over to me.

Placing my first bet, I put a thousand dollars in chips on the table before looking up at the dealer. I prayed that I would get lucky today. I needed this money, and this was the only thing I knew I could do to get it. He dealt the cards. "Fourteen," he called out.

I looked at the cards before looking back up at the dealer. "Hit me."

He placed another card on the table. "Eighteen."

"Hit me again," I spoke.

Shit, it was all or nothing. The dealer placed the card down onto the table, a two of diamonds. 'Twenty," the dealer called out.

I watched as I waited for the dealer to flip over his card. He flipped it. A six of hearts appeared, giving him sixteen. He had no choice but to deal himself another card. Nine of clubs, a bust. He slid my winnings over to me before I placed yet another thousand dollar bet. The dealer dealt the cards. A ten of clubs and an ace of spades.

"Blackjack!" the dealer called out as he once again slid my winnings over to me.

I smirked, already seeing this was about to be a great night. Feeling good, I decided to up my bet. Placing two thousand in chips onto the table, I smiled, looking up at the dealer, waiting for him to deal the cards and pass over my winnings. His card, an ace of hearts, my card, a three of diamonds. He flipped over my card, a two of clubs, giving me five in total. A low ball on a two thousand dollar bet. I didn't let him see me sweat, just calmly told him to hit me. A ten of spades. *Fifteen, shit!* I placed my hand up, letting the dealer know that I would stand.

He flipped his card. "Blackjack!"

After losing the two thousand, I decided to lower my bets to five hundred. I played for what seemed like hours before I had a total of ten thousand dollars. Standing up from the table, knowing it was time for me to cash out, I began making my way up to the teller. The lines weren't too long, and I walked up behind a dark-skinned, older man with low cut, salt and pepper hair. He was the next person in the shortest line to see a teller.

He walked up, and I couldn't help but hear that he was turning in fifty thousand in chips. Damn, I wish I had one of those days again. Grabbing his money, the man nodded at me before walking away. I cashed in, made my way to the car, and went home.

I knew that tomorrow, I would be right back at it, playing that same five thousand and seeing how much I could get. Although I'd doubled my money, it still wasn't enough, and if my winnings continued to be low, the entire week would go by, and I still wouldn't have enough to get Braylen back. That was something that I couldn't let happen.

When I arrived back home, I immediately went into my room, counted out five thousand dollars, and placed it inside of an empty shoebox at the top of my closet.

I placed the other thousand on my nightstand, so it would be ready for me tomorrow when I went back to the casino. Pulling my phone from my jean pocket, I called Braylen. My blood boiled when she still didn't answer. I called her back at least three dozen times, only for her voicemail to answer them all.

Pissed, I walked into the bathroom and took the bandage off of my hand before getting into the shower. When I was done, I dried off and rewrapped my hand. Putting on a pair of black hoop shorts, I went down into the living room and turned on the TV. I had no desire to be in my room if Braylen wasn't there with me.

Chapter Seven

BANKS

Braylen and I walked back into the house after our Target run. I told her I had some work to do in my office and would be in there for about an hour. With there being many things she could do on the estate, I knew she would find something to occupy her time. I watched as she walked up the stairs before I made my way to my office.

Taking my seat at my desk, I opened my laptop, powering it on before putting in my password. It had been an entire twenty-four hours since the last time I was at my desk, and I hoped someone had found the missing girl. If she got away and opened her mouth to anyone, it could bring heat down on my operation. The first thing I noticed was there were three new messages in my contractor folder. Those messages would just have to wait as I double clicked on my inbox to see if I had any new messages. I bit my bottom lip when I saw there were none.

No message meant no word. They hadn't found her yet. She was still out there, able to wreak havoc on everything I'd worked so hard for. Pissed, I sent a private email to my three top lieutenants, letting them know we would be having a meeting at eight o'clock. There was no need for me to give the location. They already knew how these meetings went. The coverup, a dinner party amongst friends. Everyone had dates, and tonight, mine would be Braylen. It was the perfect cover up just in case anyone was watching. Opening my contractor folder, I read each message before finding the perfect match for each.

Once I was done, I placed a call to Sabrina, letting her know that I needed clothes for both Braylen and me for our night out. She agreed, letting me know she would be over within the hour. I placed another call, this time to Ayanna. She twisted me up once a week, and I knew she was cold with doing hair. I wanted Braylen to look and feel beautiful tonight. While this would be work for me, it would be pleasure for her.

———

Sabrina arrived exactly an hour later, walking inside with a smile. Her heels clicked against the floor with each step she took. She let me know she had everything in her car and would need someone to get it for her. Nodding my head, I texted Zeek, letting him know to have everything brought in and taken to the master bedroom.

"I hope y'all ready to make a power play because I brought war clothes," Sabrina spoke, giving me a wink.

We walked up the stairs, and I went down the hall to Braylen's room. She was sitting in one of the accent chairs by her window. I told her to come with me, and she immediately got up and walked over to me without saying a word. I grabbed her hand and guided her to my bedroom.

"What's all this?" she asked, looking at all the clothing items Sabrina brought with her.

"We have a dinner party to attend tonight. Sabrina is going to get us ready."

"A'zir, we can start with you since you're probably gonna be the easiest," Sabrina spoke, walking over to one of the clothing racks and beginning to pull things down. "Let's see how you look in this."

"A'zir? Is that your real name?" Braylen asked, looking over at me.

I nodded my head yes. Only a few people knew my government name and even fewer called me by it. Sabrina just so happened to be one of those people.

"I like it." She smiled.

"Thank you."

I took off my shirt and joggers right there, leaving on nothing but my black cotton boxers. I saw the way Braylen looked over at my exposed chest, and I smirked. I put on the black Rick Owens suit and the black button up Balmain shirt that Sabrina handed me. I took a look in my full-length mirror, admiring the way the suit looked on my body.

"This is perfect."

"Good. You can pair it with these Maison Margiela loafers." She handed me the shoes before turning to look at Braylen. "Now it's your turn."

Sabrina handed Braylen a black Alexander McQueen gown. The moment she put it on, it looked like the dress was made just for her. The gown dipped low in the front and clung to every curve she had. I licked my lips when I saw the split that ran up her thigh. She smiled at me, and I knew that meant she liked the dress. Her shoes and bag were McQueen as well. Sabrina had come in and got us together quickly.

About five minutes after Sabrina left, Ayanna and her team were coming in. Since I'd just gotten a fresh retwist, her and her team would be in charge of hair and makeup for Braylen. I knew this was something that would take a couple of hours, so I decided to go for a swim while I waited. Grabbing a pair of swimming trunks from my drawer, I wrapped my locs up and made my way down to the indoor pool.

I peeled out of my clothes, setting them inside a chair, before stepping down into the pool. The water was warm, and I dipped under, allowing the water to cover me. I swam slow laps around the pool, allowing the water to become therapy to my body. The girl they'd lost was really getting to me, and I knew if I didn't calm down before I went to this meeting. I might do something I would regret later. Swimming was the way to do so. While I was in the water, I knew I had total control, even if I didn't have control of the situation at hand.

I swam several more laps before getting out the pool and heading up to my room to shower. When I was done, I dried off before oiling my body. Once I was dressed, I placed my plain gold Rolex around my wrist and a single chain around my neck. When I was done, I sprayed myself with Mason Margiela's Replica Jazz Club from head to toe. Looking at my watch, I saw it was six thirty, and it was time for us to go. Walking out the room, I headed to Braylen. Placing my hand on the knob, I opened the door before walking in.

I smelled her before I saw her. She was wearing Baccarat, and it smelled amazing on her. She walked into view and nearly took my breath away. If I thought she looked beautiful in the dress when she tried it on, that was nothing compared to the way she looked now. The dress framed her every curve.

Her hair was pinned up in a curly bun with a few loose strands framing her face. She looked like perfection. Her deep brown eyes locked with mine, and suddenly, all I could think about were her soft moans. Thoughts of what I was going to do to her when we got back home played in my head.

"You look beautiful," I complimented, walking toward her.

I trailed my fingers up her arm and over her collarbone. Her skin was as soft as silk. Something this smooth should be forbidden. I couldn't wait to feel her body on mine. If this party wasn't a business meeting, I would have said fuck it and undressed her right here and now. However, business first, fucking the shit out of Braylen immediately after.

"Thank you," she replied with a smile. I took her hand into my mine, leading her down the stairs and out to my SUV where Zeek was waiting.

The house whispered old money. Ducked off on the westside of Detroit in Palmer Woods, it was a four bedroom three-bathroom brick house that I'd purchased three years ago. I had the house fully furnished, and it was used for our business meetings. Only myself and my three lieutenants had the address and the access codes. Zeek stopped the car and opened the doors for Braylen and I to exit. The cars that were parked in the circular driveway let me know that everyone had already arrived. Taking Braylen by the hand, I led her up the steps, put in the code, and opened the door. The entryway had polished marble leading to the hardwood flooring throughout. A frosted glass chandelier that hung above us lit the area. The walls were gray, lined with black and white abstract paintings and a few chrome sculptures.

I heard voices coming from the living room, and I led Braylen inside. Malik stood against the edge of the marble fireplace in a cream suit. He stood six foot two with dark skin and a full beard. He looked like a regular businessman; however, he was anything but. Malik was the person you called when you wanted someone gone for good. He was the best at his job and had more bodies on him than a cemetery. On his arm was Imani, a slim, brown skinned beauty with an hourglass silhouette. Her face looked like she'd just stepped off a runway in Paris, and she always smelled good every time I saw her.

Tariq sat on the black sofa in a gray suit. He was light skinned with a bald head, making him look like Suge Knight. He was head of security and for good reason. Next to him sat his girlfriend, Savannah. They had been together for years, and she was the only female that any of us brought around that knew exactly what we did. She was a honey brown diva that commanded the attention of whatever room she walked inside. Her red dress was tight and strapless, and her hair was in huge curls down her back.

DeShawn sat in a chair across from the couch. He was Malik's brother and two years younger than the rest of us. At just twenty-four, he was smarter than a lot of men twice his age. He had coffee colored skin and a head full of waves. He wore a navy suit with a white shirt and a pair of black loafers. His girlfriend, Jade, sat on his lap wearing a long black dress. I introduced Braylen to everyone before suggesting we go into the dining room.

The dark wood table was already set for eight, and we all took our seats. We were served by Chef Lou and his team, who brought out our first course, which was lobster bisque. After that came lamb chops that had been marinated for hours in several herbs and spices laid over garlic mashed potatoes and asparagus spears. The meal was delicious just as I knew it would be.

When dinner was over, me and my business partners left the table and headed down to the basement to talk. I closed the door, allowing the basement to become completely soundproof while we had our meeting. Savannah had started a conversation with the women, keeping them occupied, while we handled business. A custom steel table set in the middle of the floor with four black leather chairs around it.

Malik, Tariq, and I all took our seats while DeShawn walked right over to his touchpad that was embedded into the wall. He tapped on it several times before pulling up surveillance feeds throughout the city of Miami. I'd paid the right people good money to have cameras in all the blind spots of each city I did business out of, as well as private access to traffic cameras, facial recognition pings, and burner phone triangulation.

"Man, how the fuck they let that girl get away? I hope you fired they ass, Banks." Tariq loaded his custom Glock like he was about to kill everyone that had something to do with the missing girl. "This shit too sloppy for me," he continued.

"I don't know what the hell they were doing, but after this, a lot is about to change," I replied.

Malik sat in his chair, not saying a word, as he waited on us to tell the next move. He rode with us in whatever we did. His strength was being a chameleon. He was able to adjust to anything and put in the work to get it done.

"She couldn't have gone far. She on foot, right?" Malik asked.

"As far as I know."

"I've already flagged shelters, clinics, and just about anywhere with free Wi-Fi," Deshawn informed.

"What's the plan once we locate her?" Tariq asked, looking over at me.

"Well, once we locate her, then we send one of our people out there to go get her. We can allow them to handle her how they see fit once they have her. My only concern right now is getting her back."

"We can't trust any of the people out of Miami anymore, at least not anyone that worked at that warehouse. This one mistake could take down our entire operation," Malik spoke.

I knew he was right. Every man over that warehouse had made poor decisions that could come back on us. "What do you suggest we do, Malik?"

"DeShawn and I should go down to Miami. The two of us can locate her and bring her back. We then pull other men from other warehouses across Florida to work at the Miami location because we gotta take them niggas out. They know too much, so we can't just fire them."

"Yeah, I agree with that. But I'm going with y'all though," Tariq agreed.

I nodded my head, knowing that was the best way to ensure we kept our operation airtight. With that, we ended the meeting. Walking back upstairs, I walked into the living room to find Braylen laughing and talking with the other ladies. We stayed and all had a drink together before Braylen and I went out to my SUV and headed home.

Chapter Eight

BRAYLEN

I walked into my room and immediately took off my shoes. They were cute as hell but were not made to be worn for hours. My dress was the next to come off. Walking over to the nightstand, I took my phone out and found I had over fifty missed calls from Kyrie. Banks had already told me that I wasn't to speak to him while I was in his home, and I didn't want to. I had nothing to say to Kyrie, so there was no need for me to talk to him at all. Opening my text messages, I read all thirty-two that Kyrie sent before closing the app and placing my phone back into the nightstand.

Walking into the bathroom, I stood at the sink and washed the makeup from my face before getting into the shower. The hot water felt good against my skin as I washed every part of my body. When I got out, I dried off and rubbed myself down with shea butter. I couldn't help but wonder if Banks was coming into my room tonight. My question was quickly answered when I walked out the bathroom and saw him leaning against the wall in my room.

He didn't say a word, just stood there, holding a black, leather bag. The bag was unzipped halfway, and even from across the room, I could see what was inside. Straps, cuffs, metal clips, rope, and a few things I didn't even recognize. My breath caught in my throat as I looked at the items. His eyes ran down my body slowly and deliberately. Banks was all the way across the room, yet I could feel his touch with his glance.

"Do you remember the safe word?" he asked, just as he'd done the night before.

"Yes, I remember."

He nodded his head and walked over to me, bag still in hand. With his free hand, he grabbed the back of my neck, pulling me into him before kissing me passionately. I didn't know if he meant for the kiss to feel like that, but it caused my entire body to shudder. Moving his hand from the back of my neck to the front, he raised my head before licking up my neck. Wetness pooled between my legs as I bit my lip.

He tossed the bag onto the bed before pulling out a pair of black handcuffs. My heart began to beat rapidly, but my feet were frozen in place. I was both terrified and intrigued all at the same time. He turned back to me and ordered me to get onto the bed. I did without question. I laid back, heart pounding, breaths fast, as he guided my wrists to the headboard. He placed me in the handcuffs, and I seemed to get wetter with each click.

"Are you scared?" he whispered, lips slightly touching my ear with each word.

I nodded my head yes.

"Good."

He slowly trailed his hand up my body, admiring every inch. Banks took his time, making sure to touch every part of me. There was no urgency in his movements. Each step was calculated because he was a man that knew exactly what he wanted. Walking back over to the leather bag, Banks pulled out a black satin blindfold. Climbing over me, he slipped the blindfold over my eyes, leaving me in total darkness.

"Do you trust me?"

"No," I answered truthfully.

He placed his fingers between my legs, feeling the juices that flowed. "Your body does though."

He pressed his lips against my chest, softly kissing me. His mouth moved lower, leaving a trail of kisses on my skin and causing me to drag out a soft moan. He didn't stop, just continued kissing me. When he got to my belly button, I felt the coldness; it was ice. He placed the ice on my belly button before sucking it back into his mouth. The coldness from the ice and the heat of his mouth caused my body to shiver.

He continued trailing my body with kisses. He placed one of my legs up and rested it on his shoulder as he kissed the inside of my thigh, licking and sucking it gently. Banks bit down on my thigh – not hard but it caused me to gasp. I heard him chuckle before he kissed my love button and placed my leg back on the bed.

I felt him stand from the bed before I heard him rummaging through the bag again. With the blindfold on, all my other senses had been heightened. Banks walked around the bed before rubbing my clit with two fingers. My legs opened for him, and when he leaned down and kissed it softly, I moaned. After his lips came the vibrator, pressing it against me firmly. I jerked, causing the handcuffs to crackle against the headboard. I bit my bottom lip as he ran the vibrator up and down my slit. Banks increased the speed, and my moans grew louder.

"Who do you belong to?" Banks asked.

I didn't speak. What was I supposed to say? I was a married woman, so I obviously belonged to my husband. Me not answering caused him to increase the speed of the vibrator yet again. He asked once more, and I still didn't answer. This time, I felt something cool against my nipple. It wasn't ice. It felt like some type of metal. When it clamped down onto my nipple, I yelped, biting my bottom lip while still refusing to answer his question. Banks showed no mercy, placing another clip onto my other nipple before letting it go, causing it to clamp down.

"Fuckkkkkk!' I screamed out.

This was torture – pleasurable torture but torture nonetheless. Did I want him to stop? Hell no! The safe word we'd set was nowhere near coming from my lips. Neither was me telling Banks that I belonged to him. I could tell he was challenging me, but what he didn't know was that I was up for the challenge. He turned the vibrator up to the highest setting, holding one of my legs tightly so that I couldn't close them. I could feel my orgasm approaching, and Banks must have sensed it as well because he turned off the vibrator.

A few short moments later, he was climbing on top of me. His body heat pressed against mine like a weighted blanket. He kissed me once more, and our tongues danced. He kissed each of my nipples, clips still on them. Without warning, he inserted his manhood inside of me. I screamed out, arching my back and allowing him entry. His strokes were deep, and I bit my lip, taking every inch of him.

Banks rose to his knees. Grabbing my legs, he placed both of them onto his shoulders, going deeper. I wanted to grab him, pull him down on top of me, and feel his skin on my body. However, the handcuff prevented that. Banks grabbed my hips, thrusting harder, causing my breasts to jiggle. My arms stretched as the handcuffs forced them into place. I could hear Banks' grunts, and he stroked me so deep that I swore I felt it in my stomach.

Banks pulled out of me, scooting back before pushing my legs up farther. "I'm going to ask you one more time. Who do you belong to?"

No words left my lips, and I heard Banks chuckle. He pushed my legs all the way back, both feet now touching the headboard. "Oh, okay," he spoke before letting go of my legs, causing them to hit the bed carelessly. I felt him get off the bed, and I became confused. I heard him going through the bag again and returning to the bed a few moments later. One by one, he placed my legs toward the headboard, placing handcuffs around my ankles before cuffing each one to the headboard.

I felt him get back onto the bed, and he began using his tongue to massage my love button. I heard the vibrator click on again as he slid it inside me. The vibrations mixed with the soft flutters of his tongue caused my juices to flow like a river. When he moved his tongue from my clit to my ass, I came like never before. Pulling his tongue from my backside, I felt him sit up before feeling the head of his manhood on my rear opening before pushing it inside. I screamed in pain; however, a few strokes later, it was pure pleasure.

Never once did I give up from the challenge Banks had set forth by saying the safe word. Nor did I tell him that I belonged to him. I took every inch of him like a champ and almost dared him to take shit further. When we were done, Banks uncuffed me, placed everything back into the black, leather bag, and once again left without a word.

Chapter Nine

BANKS

I walked back into my master suite and went straight to the bathroom. Fucking Braylen had taken my mind off things for a moment, now here my mind was racing again. I knew Malik said they could handle it, but everything in me was telling me to go with them. I turned on the shower before stepping inside. I allowed the hot water to run down my body. Did I want to leave Braylen? Not at all. However, I felt I might have to. I'd made it this far in the business I was in because I always followed my first mind. My first mind was telling me to go with them.

Grabbing my washcloth, I lathered it before washing Braylen's scent off of me. Once out the shower, I wrapped a towel around me and walked into the bedroom area. Grabbing my phone, I placed a call to Malik. I didn't care that it was almost two in the morning. I needed to let him in on the change of plans. He answered sleepily.

"I'm going with y'all to Miami. I'm going to have the pilot have the PJ ready for five-thirty. Let Riq and D know."

"I got you."

I then placed a call to my pilot, letting him know the time I needed him to have the plane ready. He agreed with no question. Hanging up, I set an alarm for four before shooting a text to Zeek, telling him to be out front at four forty-five. I placed my phone on the nightstand before crawling into bed for the two hours I had to sleep. My alarm seemed to go off the moment my head hit the pillow.

I dressed in a pair of black joggers and a black tee. I placed my locs into a ponytail before grabbing a black leather bag from my closet. I put everything I would need for the trip inside my bag – two custom Glock nineteens, a tactical knife, black, nitrile gloves, a few flashlights, and a backup blade just in case. Zipping up the bag, I grabbed it and walked out the room. Walking into my kitchen, I left a quick note to Braylen with a rose on the kitchen counter before walking out the house.

By ten after five, I was on the tarmac, looking at the floodlights as the private jet waited for us to board. We left Detroit at exactly five thirty with nothing but business on our minds. I knew the moment we got off the plane that we needed to get right to work. I'd sent out emails for overseers from Orlando, Tampa, and Tallahassee to meet us at the Miami warehouse. They didn't know that was where they would now be working, but they would soon find out.

We touched down in Miami at exactly nine-fifteen. The humidity punched me in my face the moment I stepped off the plane. Thankfully, two black SUVs were already there, waiting on us. Deshawn and Malik got in one, peeling off quickly to find the missing girl, while Tariq and I got in the other, headed to the warehouse to drop some bodies.

We pulled up to the warehouse a little after ten. From the outside, it looked like it had been dead for decades. There were boards on all the windows, rust creeping up the siding, and tons of weeds swallowing the cracked concrete parking lot. This was the kind of place you would drive past and not look at twice. It was just how I liked it, ducked off and quiet. However, once you stepped inside, it was a different world.

The inside was organized and clean with hidden electricity. LED floodlights lined the ceiling, while two metal staircases spiraled up to the catwalk that overlooked the main floor. Soundproof panels lined the walls, and there were surveillance cameras throughout the entire building. This wasn't a hideout; it was a holding tank. Me and my partners alone were responsible for over twenty-five percent of the missing people around the country, and this was home for several of them.

Glass walled rooms lined one side of the building like makeshift cells, with only a twin sized bed and a bucket inside them. Each one of them were reinforced and heavily secured, which was supposed to make it impossible for anyone to get away. Yet someone had. The overseers had two jobs, feed the people three times a day and make sure nobody escaped. They couldn't even do that shit right.

There was no need for any meetings. I didn't care what any of them had to say. They all had to go – and now. Tariq went to the left, and I went to the right. I saw one of the overseers sitting at a desk, watching the cameras. He greeted me with a head nod as I approached him. Walking behind him as though I was coming to watch the cameras, I sliced his throat in one swift motion. I heard Tariq's gun go off twice, and I knew he'd just dropped two bodies. I moved through the aisles slowly. I caught two more in the bathroom. The bullets I put in the back of their heads dropped them both instantly. Walking out the bathroom, I met Tariq on the catwalk.

"I took down six," Tariq informed, looking around for the rest of the overseers.

"I took down three."

"Then it's one left."

The moment the words left my mouth, I saw Trig emerge. He must have heard the commotion because he came out swinging, Uzi in hand. He sprayed freely, bullets landing everywhere. Tariq and I both ducked for cover as we waited on him to run out of bullets.

"I got him!" I yelled out to Tariq.

I edged left, crawling down the staircase. Trig was too busy yelling and firing aimlessly to notice me. This right here was probably how the girl got away in the first place. None of these niggas watched their surroundings. Walking up behind him, I held up my Glock before firing one shot into his head, dropping him instantly. Tariq walked out from behind a desk, putting his gun back into his waistline before lighting a cigarette.

"I'll call the clean-up crew," he informed, taking a deep drag from his cigarette.

***

The bodies had to still be warm when the clean-up crew pulled up just minutes later. Three black Suburbans rolled in like a small funeral procession, tires crunching over the gravel. Six men walked inside swiftly, wearing gloves and black jumpsuits. There was no talking or hesitation, just the calculated steps of men who had a job to do. The smell of blood had started to settle into the concrete and clung to the air like smoke. Tariq oversaw the clean-up crew, making sure they cleaned up every inch. I watched as they zipped up body bags and began taking them outside.

About forty-five minutes later, the other crews started rolling in. They lined their cars up in the back of the warehouse, getting out the cars and walking inside. They all stood there with the same quiet respect. There were no questions. Every answer was written in blood and bullet holes. I stood in the middle of the warehouse as they all gathered.

"This is y'all new location," I spoke, voice low but sharp. "These muthafuckas slipped up. And this is what happens when muthafuckas slip up. Let this be a lesson to all of you."

No one argued or said anything for that matter, not one murmur of resistance. Before I could say another word, my phone buzzed. Reaching into my pocket, I noticed it was Deshawn.

"D, what up doe?"

"We got her. Found her ass hiding out at one of them rinky dink ass motels. We on our way back right now. GPS says fifteen minutes."

I exhaled. Finally, some good news. "Cool, we almost done here too. Once y'all bring her back, we can head back to the PJ."

"Cool, see you in a minute."

Malik and Dashawn pulled up exactly fifteen minutes later. The girl was with them; however, she was passed out, and Malik had her thrown over his shoulder, walking her inside. He took her to her room, placing her into her bed, before closing and locking the door.

"Y'all ready to get the hell outta here?" Malik asked.

"Fuck yeah. I got shit to do back home," I replied.

From the moment I'd left the house, Braylen had been on my mind. I never intended to leave her. I had no intentions on doing any business aside from what I could do at home the entire week she was there. However, this was something I had to do. I hoped she had a good day and got some much-needed relaxation. I had something planned for us tonight that I hoped she'd enjoyed. Braylen was a queen and should be treated as such. The problem was that she didn't know it. I wanted to show her, but her vision was clouded by insecurities and a bum ass nigga.

"Yeah, I bet you do. That thick ass chick you brought to the meeting last night. I bet yo ass thought I wasn't gon' say nothing," Tariq joked.

"I ain't gon' lie. I was gon' ask you who she was. Where you meet her?" Deshawn asked.

"Damn, y'all niggas nosy as fuck. Can a nigga live? I don't never ask y'all about the bitches y'all bring wit y'all. Malik got a new bitch with him damn near every other meeting. I don't be saying shit. I bring a new bitch to a meeting, and now y'all jumping down my damn throat."

"Last new bitch you brought to a meeting was Kamaria. She been yo date to every meeting for the past year. So, yes, you bringing this new chick is something to talk about," Malik spoke as the four of us walked toward the warehouse door.

"Damn. Fuck is this, drill Banks' day?"

"Hell yeah, nigga. Now tell us what's up." Tariq blinked.

"Braylen's husband owed me some money. Instead of me killing him, he offered me her for a week, and I accepted," I answered truthfully. These were my homies. We were more like brothers than colleagues. If I could be honest with anyone, it was them.

"Nigga, what? Her husband gave her to you for a week? Hell nah, couldn't be me." Tariq laughed.

"Shit, that's because Banks be out here puttin' the fear of God in these niggas," Deshawn uttered, cracking a smile.

"Man, chill out. Her husband couldn't pay, so he offered her. I ain't have shit to do with that. Him offering her is one thing, but the fact that she actually went along with it is what's crazy to me."

"Yeah, homegirl either really love her man or she hella insecure. Maybe even a little bit of both. You betta watch out for her. She could be more than you bargained for," Deshawn warned.

I brushed it off, ready to get back home and back to her. She'd taken last night like a champ, not calling out the safe word at all. I'd turned it up a notch while still taking it easy on her. Tonight wouldn't be the same. I'd made up a safe word for a reason, and I was determined to make her say it.

The four of us separated once we got to the SUVs, two of us in each just as before. We made our way to the airport and boarded the private jet. Seeing how I hadn't gotten a lot of sleep the night before, I took the flight home as a chance to do so.

Chapter Ten

KYRIE

The sun was barely up when I opened my eyes. Rolling over to look at the clock on the nightstand, it was seven-thirty. My sleep had become nonexistent without Braylen. Picking up my phone, I saw there were no missed calls or texts, which meant no word from Braylen. I opened our text thread, making sure that each one of my texts had been sent. When I saw that her read receipts were on and that she'd read all my messages, my blood boiled. I called her five more times, each one of them going to voicemail.

Tossing the covers off of me, I walked into the bathroom, handling my morning routine. When I was done, I made my way to the kitchen. I knew Braylen was upset with me for forcing her to go with Banks. I knew this was my fault, so I couldn't be mad at anyone but myself. This was on me, and only I could fix it. I knew once I got the money and got my baby back, everything would go back to normal.

Opening the fridge, I grabbed a carton of eggs, a pack of turkey bacon, and a tube of biscuits. I placed the biscuits onto a baking sheet before placing them into the oven. I then heated up a pan before placing some butter and a few slices of turkey bacon inside. Once that was done, I scrambled my eggs. Pouring myself a glass of orange juice, I took my plate to the table and sat down to eat. I was on a mission, and I wasn't going to allow my feelings of what my wife might be doing get in the way of that.

Once I was done eating, I washed my dishes before heading up to my bathroom to take a shower. I needed to start my day early, so I could get as much money as I could. When I was done, I dried off and put on a pair of jeans and a black t-shirt. I'd forgot to tie my braids down the night before, so my hair was more of a mess than it already was. Picking up my brush, I brushed them back before putting on my shoes. I grabbed my wallet, the five thousand dollars, and the keys to Braylen's car before leaving the house and making my way back to Greektown Casino.

I immediately walked over to the Blackjack table and took a seat. I placed the five thousand dollars on the table and received my chips in return. I knew I needed to win big today because I needed my baby back home with me where she was supposed to be. I placed my first bet, this time starting low with only five-hundred-dollar bets. I needed luck to be on my side today because I didn't want to spend another night without Braylen.

Hand after hand, I piled up my money. I didn't know how long I'd been at the table, but it felt like hours. Feeling as though I'd done all I could for the day, I got up and walked away. Twelve thousand dollars wasn't nearly enough. I contemplated taking the five thousand back to the table and trying to make some more. However, I thought twice about it, not wanting to risk the chance of losing the money altogether.

I turned to walk out of the casino, and that was when I saw him, the old man from yesterday. He stood there, leaning against a slot machine. His eyes were hidden behind dark glasses, but I knew it was him. He looked to be staring at me; however, I couldn't tell or be sure. When I began to walk away and the man followed me, I knew for sure he was looking at me. Not knowing what the man wanted, I began walking faster. The last time I was followed from a casino, I was robbed. Shit, if you asked me, that was the reason I was in this situation now. I had to make it to my car with the money in my pocket because there was no way I was going to have a repeat of that day.

"You play like a man with purpose," he called out, his voice as smooth as Jazz after midnight. "You won't find what you looking for in this place though. Not the kind of money you want to make and not the way you trying to make it."

I stopped. I turned to look at him but didn't speak. The man walked closer to me before speaking again. "If you want to make some real money and change your life, you'd follow me."

My eyes narrowed. "Follow you where?"

"If you follow me, then you will find out." The man walked over to his car, which was parked a few spots away from me. I nodded my head, getting into my car and following the man out of the parking structure.

A few minutes later, we pulled up to a Coney Island not too far from the casino. Once the old man got out his car, so did I, and we both walked into the diner and grabbed a table.

"You ready to talk business, youngblood?" he asked the moment we sat down.

"Um, can you at least tell me what your name is first?"

"It's Vic." He chuckled. "I guess I should have led with that."

A waitress walked to the table, and Vic ordered two coffees before she walked away.

"What's the business?"

"I watch people. I've been doing so for a long time, and I'm rather good at it. I've watched you at the table at different casinos, and I bet you never even noticed me. I noticed you though. The way you play and how often you play." Vic leaned in closer, lowering his tone before speaking again. "I count cards, probably been doing it since you been born. I'm putting together a small team, three maybe four, to hit the downtown casinos in rotation. Nothing loud and flashy though, just in and out."

I blinked, looking over at him. "You serious?"

"I'm too old to lie."

"And you think I'm just gon' jump in on that?"

"What I think is that you got something to do and clearly don't have the money to do it or else you wouldn't be in the casino everyday trying to make some money."

He was right. I needed to get Braylen back. "What's the cut?"

"Depends on the take. But I can tell you that you gon' make a lot more in a week with me than you would by yoself."

I sat back in my seat, processing everything Vic was saying to me. This wasn't just a nickel and dime hustle. This was the blueprint to a system. This could set me up good for a long time; however, it was also risky. I'd heard horror stories about old gamblers that had been caught counting cards. It wasn't illegal, but if caught, the police were the furthest thing from your mind. I heard a story about one man where the casino owner cut off his hand for counting cards. That was drama I wanted no parts of.

"Have you ever been caught?" I asked Vic.

"Not one time in all my years."

I nodded. Vic slid a folded napkin over to me with an address and time written on it. "Training begins tomorrow. Be there on time if you serious about making some money."

I stared down at the napkin, Braylen's face flashing through my mind, and I nodded my head. Placing the napkin into my pocket, I stood up and walked out the diner.

Chapter Eleven

BRAYLEN

I woke up to the sun shining through my open curtains. Rolling over and looking at the clock, I saw that it was eight-fifteen. I stretched under the covers, the inside of my thighs aching from what Banks had done to my body the night before. My back was sore as hell, but I had taken that shit like a fucking champ. I'd taken every painful pleasure and liked it. I could tell I had fucked his mind up when I wouldn't tell him I belonged to him. What Banks didn't know was that I was just as good at the art of seduction as he was.

Getting out of the bed, I walked into the bathroom to relieve myself. Banks had done it again, fucked the shit out of me, and once again, he was the first thing on my mind. I could only wonder if I was the first thing on his. Walking over to the shower, I turned it on, allowing it to become steamy before stepping inside. The hot water rushed over my skin, easing the soreness in my muscles.

I leaned my forehead against the cool shower tile, closing my eyes. Visions of Banks on top of me flashed through my mind. What the fuck was happening in my life? Here I was, a married woman whose husband had sold her to this man. Banks. Just his name alone sent shivers throughout my entire body. My body wanted him. I wanted him.

Twenty minutes later, I stepped out the shower. Wrapping a towel around myself, I walked into the bedroom area and grabbed my phone from the nightstand. The first thing I noticed was the thirty missed calls, all from Kyrie. Vita had called me twice as well as texted. Calling her back, I placed the phone to my ear.

"Bitch, where the fuck have you been?" Vita yelled into the phone. "Last time we talked, you got off the phone quick as hell. Telling me you would call me back. Not only did you not call me back, but you wasn't even answering yo phone. I go over yo house, and Kyrie looks like he got the dawg shit beat outta him, and yo ass nowhere to be found. What the fuck is going on? Bitch, if you need help, press two!"

I knew Vita would be worried about me. I usually spoke to her every day, sometimes several times a day. So, the fact that I hadn't spoken to her in days was unlike me.

"Hello? Are you okay?"

"Yeah, my bad. I'm here."

"Bray, what the fuck is going on? Something ain't right, and I'm ready to squad up and run down on Kyrie's ass. Because whatever it is, I know that nigga got something to do with it."

I paused. I could picture Vita calling her cousins and running up on Kyrie to find me. That was the type of friend she was. So, I knew once I told her what was going on, she would be ready to damn near kill him.

"Yeah, Kyrie has been fuckin' up lately with all his gambling."

"Lately? Name a time that he wasn't fucking up. That nigga is a fuck up. His daddy was a fuck up too, let his mama tell it. Shit and his granddaddy. He the third generation of an ain't shit nigga. Please don't make a fourth, Bray."

"I gotta tell you something." I spoke in a low tone, almost ashamed of what I was about to say.

"Bitch, please don't tell me that yo ass is pregnant." I could hear the disappointment in her voice.

"No, fool, ain't nobody pregnant. Can you be serious because I really have something to tell you?"

"What's up, Bray? Tell me what's going on."

I took a deep breath before speaking again. "Kyrie owes this dude name Banks a hundred thousand dollars. We both know Kyrie don't have that much money or a way to get it with all the gambling he be doing. So, he used me."

"Used you? Used you how?"

"For collateral," I whispered.

The silence became heavy, and my heart dropped. Admitting what my husband had done was horrible. The fact that I'd gone along with it was worse. I shook my head as I waited for Vita's response.

"What the fuck did you just say?"

I winced, pulling the phone away from my ear. Her voice had gone up about ten octaves.

"I know you fuckin' lying! This muthafucka put you up for what? Like he let somebody buy you like you a piece of property or some shit?"

My eyes burned, and tears threatened to fall. I blinked them away. I wasn't crying over this shit. Not anymore.

"Yeah. He owed a hundred bands; Banks was about to kill him. He cut off his finger and everything. Shit got real fucked up. He thought he was about to die, so in the last effort to save his life, he offered me."

"This dirty ass, broke ass, sorry ass, nothing ass, nine finger havin' ass nigga. What kind of muthafucka would even think to do some shit like this? I swear that nigga is lower than trash; that nigga dumpster juice!" Vita was cursing so loud and fast that I could only make out half of what she was saying.

"He's been calling me nonstop since I been here."

"Fuck him! You better not answer that bum ass nigga's calls."

"I'm not. Banks said I'm not allowed to talk to him while I'm at his house anyway."

"Not allowed? And who the fuck is Banks? Fuck that shit, Braylen. Send me yo location, and I'ma come get you."

"Nah, Vita. I gotta stay for the week."

"Braylen Nicole Parker, I am not fuckin' playing with you. Send me the location. You ain't nobody's property, and that nigga can't hold you hostage. That shit is illegal."

"He's not holding me hostage, Vee. I kinda want to be here. He might be a little mean, but just the glimpse I've gotten of his world so far got me wanting more," I confessed.

"Bitch, what?! Let me find out you over there on some fifty shades shit."

We both laughed. We stayed on the phone for a few more minutes with Vita telling me to call her if I needed her before ending the call. I sat on the bed for a moment, thinking about what Vita said. Kyrie wasn't shit, and I didn't even know if I wanted to continue on with things being this way. Kyrie would need to get some help, and we both would probably have to go to therapy if our marriage was going to work at all.

I slipped into a black, two-piece, yoga set, one of the many Banks had gotten me from Target. The material felt good on my skin, and I was glad I'd gotten them in every color they had. My hair that was once styled to perfection was now all over my head. I brushed it back into a neat ponytail before making my way down to the kitchen.

The smell of the cooked food hit my nostrils the moment I walked into the kitchen. My stomach growled. The chef had placed a steaming plate of corned beef hash, scrambled eggs, and whole wheat toast atop of the black marble counter. A cold glass of orange juice sat next to it. Right above the plate was a folded note and a single red rose. Smiling, I grabbed the rose, placing it to my nose and smelling it.

Unfolding the note, I saw it was from Banks. He let me know that he had some business to take care of and would be home later on tonight. He also said that he had something planned for us later and wanted me to get dressed once my package arrived. I smiled, taking the plate of food and the glass of juice to the table and sitting down to eat. With Banks being gone for the day, it meant I had free rein of the house.

There was so much to do here, and today would be the day I did them all. Once I was done eating, I placed my dishes into the dishwasher before heading up to my room to put on a pair of sneakers. I'd never played tennis before a day in my life, yet here I was, getting ready to head out to the court in Banks' backyard.

I found a racket the moment I walked onto the court and picked it up. This was the first time I'd even held one before, and I had no clue what I was doing. The morning air was cool, low seventies at most, but I could tell it was going to be a really hot day. The only background noise I heard was the soft chirps of the birds in the distance. There were no car horns, police sirens, or any of the chaos I was used to. It was so peaceful.

I bounced the ball a few times, using the racket the way I'd seen people do on TV. I tossed the ball up, swinging the racket recklessly, and missed the ball completely. I laughed, bouncing the ball once more, tossing it up, just to miss it again. However, this time, the ball rolled to the other side of the court. I laughed at myself, thinking about how silly I must have looked.

"Girl, ain't nobody watchin' yo ass. Just have fun." I spoke aloud as I ran across the court and retrieved the ball.

I chased after the ball, grabbing it before trying again. This time, my racket made contact with the ball, barely, but it was contact. The ball hit the ground a few feet away from the net, not going across at all, and I laughed. This was the first time I'd genuinely laughed since I'd found out that Kyrie had sold me. I liked it. I played out on the court for a couple hours, enjoying myself, until I decided to see what else I wanted to do.

Since I'd worked up a sweat on the tennis court, I decided that it was only right that my next stop would be the pool. Walking back into the house, I walked up to my room and took a two-piece, Burberry bathing suit from the drawer. Taking off my yoga outfit, I placed it inside the dirty clothes bin that set inside the en-suite bathroom.

I slipped into my bathing suit and a pair of Burberry slides Sabrina had matched with the bathing suit. Banks had two pools, an indoor and an outdoor one. I hadn't been in either of them yet, but today, I would be going to the indoor pool. The sun was only getting higher in the sky, and since I'd forgotten to get sunscreen, I would have to wait on the outdoor pool.

Walking down the stairs, I walked down the long hallway that led to the pool. The glass doors slid open automatically when I approached.

The floors were black marble – the same black marble as the kitchen countertops. It was polished so clean that I could see my reflection. The pool stretched across the room, framed by sleek, white, lounge chairs. Spotlights attached to the high vaulted ceiling danced off the water, causing it to shimmer. On the other side of the room was a huge floor to ceiling window that let in the morning light. Potted plants stood tall in each corner, giving the place a tropical, spa like vibe.

Looking around the room more, I noticed a narrow door off to the side that was cracked open just a little. I hadn't noticed it when Banks gave me the tour of the house and wanted to see what it was. Walking closer to the door opening, I saw a cedar wood filled room. *Damn, Banks, you got a sauna too?* Walking back over to the pool, I took off my slides and stepped into the water. I wasn't a very good swimmer; in fact, it had been years since I'd been in a pool. I allowed the water to cover my body. The pool was heated, and I loved the feeling of the warm water on my body.

I stayed in the water for about an hour before getting out and drying off. Once I was dry, I headed right to the sauna. Turning it on and closing the door before taking a seat, I allowed the steamy heat to ease away all my stress. In that moment, I decided to say fuck everything that was going on. Fuck Kyrie for what he'd done. Fuck the reason I was here with Banks. There were so many things around me to enjoy, and I was going to start enjoying them.

When I finally stepped out of the sauna, I felt more relaxed than ever. Walking over to the towel rack, I grabbed a towel and wrapped it around my body before slipping back into my slides and going up to my room. I walked straight to the bathroom, turning on the shower, taking my bathing suit off, and stepping right in. I took my time scrubbing every inch of my body. I washed my hair, working the thick, creamy lather through it. I allowed the water to rinse it away before repeating the process.

Getting out of the shower, I wrapped my hair in a towel before wrapping one around my body. I walked over to the mirror, plugging up the blow dryer before drying my hair. Walking back inside my bedroom, I smiled when I saw the three boxes neatly arranged on my bed with a folded note resting on top. I opened it, already knowing it was from Banks. He let me know that Ayanna and her team would be here to do my hair and makeup at three and to have everything in the boxes on by seven. I smiled, placing the note onto the nightstand, before picking up the first box.

I pulled out a high-waisted maxi skirt with a thigh high split up one side. Different shades of greens, bold orange, and gold formed a pattern over the fabric. The matching top was a structured, off the shoulder, crop top that was snatched in around the bottom. On the label, Versace. The outfit was beautiful and looked like money. Opening the other box, there were a pair of gold, Tom Ford, strappy stilettos. Banks had expensive taste, so I didn't expect anything less.

I opened the last box to see a light pink perfume bottle nestled inside. Parfums de Marly Delina. Opening the bottle, I sprayed it into the top and placed it up to my nose. The scent was soft and sweet yet seductive. I smiled, ready to see what Banks had in store for us.

I set the perfume bottle on top of the dresser, right along with the other bottles Banks had gotten me. Looking over at the clock, I saw it was one forty-five. Ayanna and her team would be here in a little over an hour. After the tennis, the swim, and the sauna, my body was tired. Walking over to the bed, I dropped my towel before stepping up into it, snuggling under the covers.

Grabbing the remote from the nightstand, I flicked on the TV that was mounted across the bed. I opened the Netflix app, scrolling until I found a movie that looked good. I laid there, watching the movie, until five to three. Getting up, I put on a navy-blue yoga two-piece just like the one I'd just taken off. The moment I got done, Zeek came to the door, letting me know that Ayanna and her team were here. I nodded my head, letting him know he could let them in.

"Hey, girl. Long time no see," Ayanna joked, seeing how I'd just met her yesterday.

She was rolling a silver suitcase behind her. Following her were two other ladies. One carried a makeup case, and the other carried a portable mirror and ring light.

"You ready to get all glammed up?" Ayanna asked with a smile.

"Yeah, I don't even know what all this is for, but I'm ready."

Ayanna flipped open the case and began pulling out several items. One of the other women motioned for me to come sit in the chair, and I did. Ayanna pulled out a long, jet-black, full lace wig on a mannequin head and a pair of tweezers and began customizing the lace while the other woman began braiding my hair. As the two of them worked, the other woman began setting up her makeup area.

When the one braiding was done, Ayanna walked over and placed a wig cap onto my head, cutting and spraying it down before gluing the wig down onto my head. She placed a black band around it before stepping out the way for a moment while the makeup artist started my face. She kept my makeup soft but luxurious. My skin was glowing like it was glass, and I knew I would need to get the name of the foundation she used. My lashes feathered out, and my lips were nude while the bronzer and highlights she used added a golden hue to my skin. By the time they were done, it was five thirty, and I looked beautiful.

Once Ayanna and her team left, I knew it was time for me to get ready. I walked over to the bed where I'd left the outfit Banks had gotten for me. I peeled out of the yoga two-piece I'd not too long ago put on, leaving me standing there in nothing. I turned and looked at myself in the mirror. I really had to start back working out. Banks had a home gym that I told myself I would utilize starting tomorrow.

Grabbing a matching black, lace panty and bra set that Banks had gotten me yesterday, I put it on before rubbing lotion all over my body. I carefully slid into the silky, high-waist skirt first, the material gliding over my legs effortlessly. The split up the leg was everything, and I loved the way my thigh peeked through it. I put the matching crop top over my head slowly, careful not to mess up my hair or makeup. I adjusted the top, smiling at how good I looked in the set. I turned around, peeking at my round backside.

Taking a seat in the chair, I put on the gold stilettos before standing to my feet. I looked in the mirror once more before spraying the perfume all over me. I placed on a pair of gold earrings and a matching gold necklace. I was loving this look, and I felt beautiful.

Ten minutes after I'd gotten dressed, my bedroom door opened, and Banks walked inside. He was wearing a cream-colored short set made from soft Italian linen. I didn't know who the designer was, but I knew it was expensive and molded to his frame. His shirt was open enough for me to see his tattooed covered chest. As always, he wore minimal jewelry. A rose gold Rolex adorned his wrist while a slim Cartier chain hung from his neck. His locs hung down past his shoulders, and I shifted in my heels.

I stood there, looking at him for several seconds, taking him all in. He looked so damn good, and I wanted to jump on him right then and there.

"You look beautiful," he complimented. "Are you ready to go?"

"Thank you. You look very handsome yourself. And yes, I'm ready."

Banks nodded, taking my hand in his and leading me out of the room. We walked outside to his SUV that was parked in front of the door. Zeek opened our doors the moment he saw us walk outside, and we both got in. We drove in silence for about twenty minutes until the car stopped. Zeek opened our doors, and when I got out, my mouth dropped.

I didn't know where I was expecting Banks to take me, but this was not it. The enormous yacht in front of me was more than just a boat. This muthafucka was a floating mansion. Three decks high, the white and gold masterpiece gleamed under the falling sun. Banks helped me onto the yacht, and the second I stepped aboard, I realized it wasn't filled with other people; it was just us.

"I rented this entire yacht just for us." Banks spoke aloud as if he could read my mind.

He guided me up to the main deck with his hand resting lightly on the small of my back. A private dining table had been set up toward the back of the deck. A white, linen tablecloth rested on the top. Crystal glasses and thin flickering candles set across from a vase filled with red roses. Two chairs set side by side, and I smiled. I looked up at Banks, heart pounding. This was the most beautiful thing anyone had ever done for me, and I couldn't believe it was actually happening.

He walked me over to the table, pulling out my chair, before I took my seat. A private chef appeared before us, holding two plates. He set them down in front of us before removing the cloches. He revealed a dinner of filet mignon, lobster tail, truffle mashed potatoes, and creamed spinach. He filled our flutes with champagne before walking away.

Banks picked up his glass and turned to me. "Let's make a toast."

I smiled, picked up my glass, and turned to look at him. "What are we toasting to?"

"To you, to us, and to the night we are about to have."

Our glasses clicked, and we both took sips. The champagne tasted light and sweet against my tongue, and I took one more sip. The food was delicious with the steak being so tender I could cut it with a fork.

"Do you like this?" Banks asked, looking over at me.

He seemed softer than he'd ever been with me. I didn't see the cold-eyed asshole that usually looked back at me. *This must be A'Zir because Banks could never be this nice.* I chuckled to myself.

"I love this, Banks. I've never been on a yacht before, and this is extremely beautiful."

We ate dinner as we watched the sunset over the water. When dinner was over, the chef came to remove our plates, and Banks stood to his feet. He offered me his hand without saying a word, and I took it on command. I stood to my feet, and he guided me around the table before pulling me close to him. My body pressed against his firm chest. Soft music played through hidden speakers, and we began to sway.

With both of his hands planted on my hips, I rested my head on his shoulder. We danced underneath the stars as the yacht swayed to the beat of the ocean. This was the safest I'd felt in days, and as we danced, I pretended this man was mine. That he was everything I'd dreamed of plus more. That I was the love of his life and the only woman that he wanted to be with. For that moment, the fact that I'd been sold to him by my own husband didn't exist, and I pretended we'd been brought together by fate to live our lives together forever.

Banks kept me pressed against him as if he felt the same way I did. The breeze whispered against my skin, cooling the steamy heat coming from between my thighs and spreading over my body. I wasn't sure how long we danced, but every minute in his arms felt like a lifetime. He pulled me in closer than I already was, which I didn't think was even possible. I didn't resist either. I wanted to be as close to him as I could get. My body molded to his effortlessly.

He leaned down, lips pressed against my ear. "Let's go inside."

I nodded before Banks laced his fingers through mine and led me across the deck. Once inside, the air changed. It was now warmer and thicker. The dim lights guided our way as we walked across the marble floors. Banks didn't stop until he got to a large, frosted glass door with golden trim. The door opened into a private room. It was a large, open space with a purple, velvet sectional that set in the middle of the room. There was large floor to ceiling windows that offered an endless view of the dark ocean and starry sky, while a heavy wood bar stocked with crystal decanters of expensive liquor set on the other side of the room.

He turned to me before pulling me closer to him. Placing his nose to my neck, he inhaled deeply. "This perfume smells really good on you."

Just the slight touch of his nose against my neck caused my juices to begin flowing from between my legs. He kissed my neck, and my entire body shivered. Placing his hand on my chin, he guided my lips to his, kissing me deeply. Our tongues dance, tangling together slowly. His hands roamed my body. Sliding them down my back, he gripped my ass tightly. I moaned softly as his fingers squeezed my backside.

He walked me over to the bar, pouring us both a small glass of brown liquor. I took a sip, and the smooth liquor ran down my throat. Banks finished his glass in one gulp. Taking the glass from my hand, he placed it down on the bar before walking me over to the window. He pressed me against the glass with his hand trailing up my thigh, gripping my skin. He moved his hand over my hip and stomach. Moving his hand up to my breasts, he gently caressed them both before continuing to move upward.

He rested his hand around my neck. There was not enough pressure to cut off my airway, but it was firm enough for me to know he was serious. He turned my head to the left, placing his mouth to my ear. "Nobody else gon' ever make you feel like this. This pussy is already mine. You show me that every time I touch you. We can work on that heart later."

Before I could respond, he dropped to his knees in front of me. He dragged my skirt upward, resting it above my hips. He placed one finger onto the thin band of my thong, pulling it and ripping it instantly before throwing it to the floor. Banks looked up at me, and the darkness in his eyes was back.

Tossing one of my legs over his shoulder, he placed his head between my thighs. His tongue moved in slow strokes around my love button. He licked me like a cold popsicle on a hot summer day. I cried out, clenching the windowsill with one hand and his locs in the other. I kept my balance on one leg as Banks devoured me passionately. He hummed against my clit; the vibration shooting up my body damn near caused me to fall. He sucked on my clit gently before swirling his tongue over it, causing my knees to buckle as my moans grew louder.

"That's it. Cum for me, baby," he whispered.

"Banks!" I screamed out as I erupted into his mouth.

Banks stood to his feet, pulling me in and kissing my lips once more. Turning me around, he placed my chest to the window before pulling my hips back toward him. Before I could even catch my breath, he was thrusting inside of me in one deep stroke. I felt the warmth of him throughout my entire body. Banks pumped in and out of me hard and fast as he kept my hips steady.

I heard Banks' grunts grow louder, and his strokes became faster. Removing one hand from my hip, he brought it down hard on my ass cheek, sending a burning sensation up the right side of my ass. I yelped.

He leaned in, still stroking me, and kissed my neck. I could tell his climax was nearing and so was mine. Before I knew it, Banks was spilling over inside of me, nestling his seeds inside my warmth.

By the time we got off the yacht, it was almost three in the morning, and I was more than tired. The car ride was quiet. The day had been long for us both. Although I enjoyed every moment, I was now ready for bed. Banks' hand rested on my thigh the entire ride home, softly showing his possessiveness. He didn't speak and didn't need to. What was understood never needed to be explained. He'd stated his claim on me, and at this point, I was ready.

When we pulled up to the house, Zeek opened our doors and let us out the car. Banks kissed me softly once we stepped inside, letting me know that he was heading up to his room to go to sleep. I smiled, knowing that I was about to do the same. I made my way upstairs, slipping off my heels one step at a time, my body still throbbing from everything Banks had done to it. When I walked inside my room, I closed the door behind me and leaned against it for a second, exhaling slowly. I couldn't believe the day I'd just had.

This morning, I was floating in his indoor pool, mind spinning over all the amenities Banks had at his disposal. Now, after the yacht, the sunset dinner, and the way he'd been fucking the shit out of me, I was on cloud nine. I smiled at the way a horrible situation was turning out to be one of the best things that had ever happened to me.

Walking into the bathroom, I turned on the shower. Steam filled the entire bathroom, and I stepped inside. The hot water hit my skin like silk, wrapping my entire body in warmth. I closed my eyes and let the water wash everything away. For the first time in a long time, I didn't feel broken. I felt more alive than ever, and I knew that Banks had everything to do with that.

Once I was out the shower, I dried off before walking back into the bedroom. I stepped into the bed, fully naked, and grabbed my phone from the nightstand drawer. Just as I suspected, Kyrie had texted and called me several dozen times. Opening our text thread, I did exactly what Banks told me not to do. I texted Kyrie.

Chapter Twelve

KYRIE

My alarm sounded, and I immediately opened my eyes. The sky outside my bedroom window was still dark. I laid there for a second, staring up at the ceiling, my heart beating fast for no reason at all. My phone rested on the nightstand, face down. I hadn't checked it since before I went to sleep last night, mainly because I knew Braylen hadn't called me. However, I grabbed it anyway. I smiled when I noticed there was a message from her.

It had been three long days since I'd heard her voice, and I needed to know she was okay. I needed for her to know how sorry I was and that I would be coming to get her soon. This situation allowed me to see that I needed to start treating my wife better. So, the moment she was back home, that was exactly what I was going to do. I quickly opened the text, eager to see what she had to say.

Braylen: Stop calling and texting me!

That was it, five little words. My hand tightened around the phone until my knuckles popped. I read it again and again, as if I was expecting the words to change as I read them. There was no way she wrote that. Braylen would never speak to me like that, not even when she was mad. I knew my wife, and I knew after all this time of not speaking, she would be sending paragraphs, not five punk ass words. This had Banks' name written all over it. That bastard had her phone. I could feel it in my gut.

83

He was controlling the situation, keeping her away from me, making her feel like I was the enemy.

I slammed the phone down so hard it bounced. I sat up, running my hand over my face. The rage boiled in my chest. I stood up, jaws clenched tightly. I'd already made the decision to meet with Vic and get in on the crew he was putting together. I had made the decision the moment he told me what he was doing but didn't confirm it to him until that night. He let me know that the training would start exactly at seven this morning, the time written on the paper and that I was not to be late.

I walked into the bathroom and turned the water on hot. Stepping out of my hoop shorts and T-shirt, I looked at my reflection in the mirror. My bruises were still all there, but the swelling had started to go down. My hand was stilled wrapped up with half of a finger missing. I looked as though I needed to be resting in bed, but instead, I was on a mission.

I stepped into the shower, scrubbing my entire body three times before getting out. After I dried off and changed my bandage, I threw on a pair of black joggers, a white T-shirt, and a pair of black Nikes. I was ready to get to the money and ready for Vic to teach me how. Heading down to the kitchen, I made myself a bowl of cereal before sitting at the table.

I checked the time. It was six twenty-six. I ate quickly, ready to get to my training session. I finished, washed my bowl, and was in the car by six forty. It was still dark outside with the sun barely peeking through. I pulled out the parking lot of my townhome and made my way to the eastside.

I pulled up at exactly six fifty-nine. There were already two cars in the parking lot. Both were black, one a Charger, the other an Escalade. Both of them clean with tinted windows and no plates. Vic stepped outside like he'd been waiting on me. He didn't say a word at first, just looked me over.

"I'm glad you showed up," he finally spoke.

"Of course I did. You know how to get that one thing I need."

He smirked. "You hungry; that's the first step. Now let's see if you can make it through the rest."

The building looked like shit from the outside – cracked windows all around, overgrown grass in the lot, and a door that was hanging by one hinge. However, once I walked into the building, it was another story. I stepped through the steel side door after Vic keyed in a code on a rust covered panel. What greeted me wasn't dust or decay.

Rows of lights lined the high ceilings, illuminating sections of the warehouse. In one section, there were weights and resistance bands and a boxing ring roped off in red and black. What caught my attention was in the center of the room – two full size Blackjack tables padded in black leather with chairs surrounding them like it was a real casino.

Vic clapped his hands once. "Fall in," he ordered before two women stepped out the corner.

"Let me introduce the squad to you," Vic continued. "We are a team, and no matter what, we work together. When we come in together, we leave together. No matter what."

The first woman to step forward was tall, probably five foot eleven. She had flawless, dark skin and braids pulled back into a tight ponytail. She wore black joggers and a navy fitted tee. A gold pendant on a skinny chain hung low around her neck. She looked like she could either outthink you and or break your neck, depending on what the situation called for.

"This is Simone," Vic introduced.

Simone looked me over with a sharp eye then nodded once. "Don't fuck our shit up and we gon' be good."

The other woman was shorter, standing about five foot five but built solid. Her hair was in a low, pixie cut, and her skin was a rich caramel tone. There were tattoos peeking out from beneath her long-sleeved shirt, and both of her nostrils were pierced with gold rings through each hole.

"This is Tasha."

Tasha stepped forward and gave me a once over. Her lips curled into a smile before she spoke. "You good? You look like you already fucked up."

"Nah, I'm good. I'm just ready to get to the money."

Vic turned to me. "Good. Grab a seat at one of the tables."

Simone, Tasha, and I sat at the table while Vic walked around the table and stood in the dealer's position.

"Today," Vic spoke, fanning a deck of cards across the table, "we're going to turn your gambling addiction into a weapon."

He pulled out another deck and began flipping cards over one by one. "We're using what's called the Hi-Lo System; that will be the count. You count every card you see on the table. Two through six, that's plus one. Seven, eight, nine, those are zero. Ten through ace are all minus one. You gon' have to keep a running count in your head."

He flipped over a three. "Plus one." He then flipped over a ten. "This means we back to zero." He flipped over a six next. "Now, the count is plus one. Are you following so far?"

"Yeah, I got it," I replied, staying sharp.

"I sure hope so. Cause when the count goes up, so does your bet. It means more high cards are left in the deck. You get a better shot at hitting Blackjack, and the dealer's more likely to bust," Vic informed.

"What if they use more than one deck?" I asked.

"They usually do. It's rare that you will see a Blackjack table running off one deck. That's why we track the true count, not only the one we see. To do that, you will divide your running count by how many decks are left. So, if your running count is plus eight and you estimate four decks left, your true count is plus two. Got it?"

We practiced for hours, Simone and Tasha never missing a beat. They were counting in their heads while sipping bottled waters. I struggled for the first few hands, getting distracted and allowing the numbers to slip through my mind. However, once I got it, I had it and was ready to go.

Card after card, round after round, we kept going. Vic brought out chips and had us play a few fake hands. After four hours, my shirt clung to my back with sweat, but I had it down packed. *Running count plus six, decks remaining, three. The true count is plus two. Time to bet heavy.* I dropped a stack of chips on the table. Vic threw down my card. Blackjack!

"So, you do know what you doing. Good shit." Vic looked at the three of us. "I think we can start taking on the real thing tonight. What y'all think about that? Y'all ready?"

"Hell yeah, let's get it," I replied.

Vic nodded his head. "Let me walk you out."

I told both Simone and Tasha that I would see them later before we walked back out to my car. Vic looked me up and down once more.

"In order to do this, you will have to look the part. Give me one second. I'll be right back."

He returned a few moments later and told me to get inside his Escalade. I was skeptical at first but got in anyway. "I'm taking you shopping," Vic announced before pulling off.

We stopped at a boutique off Woodward. We walked up to the door, ringing the buzzer before being buzzed in. We were greeted by a beautiful, light skinned, thick woman. She stood about five foot two and had a sleeve of tattoos going down both of her arms. She walked up to Vic, hugging him tightly.

"I need the hook up for my homeboy," Vic spoke.

The woman looked me over before turning back to Vic. "I got you."

Vic slapped her on the ass before she motioned for us to follow her. She led us to the back of the store to a closed door that we walked through. On the other side of the door was a red velvet sofa with a dark wood coffee table that sat in front of it. The walls were floor to ceiling mirrors, and there were several racks of clothes lined up around the room. She told us to take a seat before she began going through the items.

Forty-five minutes later, I was standing in front of the mirrored wall, staring at a different version of myself. The suit was custom dark charcoal, sleek and smooth. It was single-breasted and looked like it was made for me. She paired the suit with a pair of black Ferragamo loafers. I looked like money, something I'd never looked like once in my life.

"Now for that hair," Vic spoke. "Can you do something with that shit?" He turned to look at the woman.

"I got you. Come on, nappy," she replied.

I followed her out the room and into another. This room was smaller but set up like a barbershop. I sat down in the chair while she took out my braids. She washed and dried my hair before giving me fresh corn rows to the back. When she was done braiding, she even lined me up.

Vic looked at me, nodding his head. "Now you look like you belong at the table."

He dropped me back off at the warehouse where Braylen's car was parked. Before I got out, he leaned across the console.

"Be back here by nine tonight. This is where we will all meet. We leave at nine fifteen, and we having a meeting before, so don't be late. This ain't practice no more."

I nodded in full understanding. I stepped out, keys in hand, adrenaline already creeping up my spine. I was finally about to get my baby back, and I was ready.

By nine that night, I was back at the warehouse, listening to Vic tell us all how we had to watch each other's backs. Although counting cards wasn't illegal, it was highly frowned upon, and people would be watching. By nine fifteen on the dot, we were in Vic's black Escalade, headed toward Motor City Casino downtown. Vic was quiet behind the wheel, his eyes locked on the road. Simone sat in the front seat, legs crossed, phone in hand, swiping through something silently. Tasha and I shared the backseat, riding in silence as well.

We pulled inside the casino's parking structure about twenty-five minutes later. Vic was sure to park in a spot by the door just in case we needed to run out the building fast. We stepped out of the truck like we owned the damn casino already. Simone took the lead, her long, red dress curving to her hips as they swayed. Tasha was more reserved in her fitted black dress, her short curls pinned perfectly, lips painted a deep wine. I had on that charcoal suit Vic's friend put me in, looking real good if I did say so myself.

We walked into the casino together before separating, me with Tasha and Vic with Simone. We passed the slots and roulette wheels, knowing exactly where we were going. We walked up to the Blackjack tables. I spotted a table near a wall, sliding into a seat across from a middle-aged man, and Tasha sat next to him. The dealer greeted me with a nod, and I nodded back. A few seconds later, Vic and Simone arrived at their table across from ours, taking their seats as well.

"Black chips," I spoke, pushing a few bills forward. "Let's play."

I let the count settle into my mind. Every two through six that fell was plus one. Tens, face cards, and aces were minus one. Sevens through nines meant nothing. I kept repeating that in my head, not wanting to forget. It was simple math, but at that table, with money on the line, it felt like war. When the count went to the plus, I increased my bet.

I kept track of everything, the true count, the cards already played, the rhythm of the shuffle, the behavior of the pit bosses. I made conversation with the guy next to me when needed, cracked a dry joke now and then, just to keep shit casual. However, my focus never wavered.

We rotated tables every couple hours, making sure not to draw too much attention to ourselves. At one point, Simone tossed me a look with her eyebrows raised. I gave a small nod. She was up big and so was I. This shit felt like a rush as I won hand after hand.

At one-fifteen, I stood from a table where I'd just won five straight hands and pocketed another ten grand. By the time we cashed out, it was nearly two in the morning. We didn't leave out together. Simone went first, disappearing through the back exit. Tasha followed a few minutes later, walking out without anyone suspecting a thing. I stayed behind to finish my drink then walked out through the front like any other lucky muthafucka who'd had a good night. Vic was the last to leave, bringing up the rear.

We pulled up to the warehouse at three fifteen. We all walked to a round wood table that sat in one of the corners of the warehouse. We all placed the money we made on the table, and Vic pulled out the money machine. The machine buzzed as stacks passed through it. When we were done counting, we had a grand total of two hundred and forty-nine thousand dollars. I couldn't believe how much money we'd made just in one night. With it being split four ways, that was sixty-two thousand each.

Vic gave us all our cut of the money, keeping his stacked neatly in front of him. He let us know that we would be going to a different casino tomorrow and to all meet back at the warehouse at the same time. We all agreed before leaving. Although it was late, I decided to go to a different casino for a few hours. I counted out twenty thousand dollars and walked into the casino, quickly turning it into the rest of the money that I needed to get Braylen back.

Chapter Thirteen

BRAYLEN

I woke up the next morning to the sun peeking in through my curtains. I rolled over and looked at the clock. It was eleven in the morning. *Damn, I must have been really tired,* I thought as I realized just how late I'd slept in. Pulling the covers from my body, I set up before placing my feet on the floor. Opening the nightstand, I removed my phone before I began checking my messages and missed calls. Just as I thought, Kyrie had texted and called several times. I didn't understand why he continued to call me. It was his fault that I was even here with Banks. I'd told him to stop texting and calling me, now here he was, doing it again.

Placing my phone back into the nightstand, I walked into the bathroom to take a shower. I didn't know what the day had in store for me, but with Banks, anything was possible.

After I was done in the shower, I brushed my teeth, rubbed shea butter all over me, and walked back into the bedroom area. I put on a two-piece yoga set, this time in red, before walking down to the kitchen. Breakfast set on the table, but Banks was nowhere in sight. There was also no note like he'd left for me the morning before.

Thinking he was still inside of his room, I decided to go wake him up, so we could have breakfast together. I'd just turned around to walk out the kitchen when Zeek walked inside, startling me and causing me to jump back.

"I apologize," he spoke, placing his hand against his chest. "I didn't mean to scare you. I was just coming to tell you that Banks left this morning and won't be back until later today. I'm under strict instruction to take you wherever you'd like to go. Banks has left his credit card to assure you were able to do exactly what you wanted. When you are ready, the car will be waiting."

"Thank you, Zeek." I smiled, grabbing my plate of French toast, eggs, and fresh fruit and taking it to the table before I sat down to eat.

I had no clue where I wanted to go or what I wanted to do. Everything was already here on Banks' estate. I sat there, eating my breakfast, trying to decide what I was going to do next. When I was finished, I rinsed my plate before placing it into the dishwasher. I walked up the stairs toward my room, still thinking about what I wanted to do with the day. Walking inside, I closed the door behind me before taking a seat on the bed.

What did I want to do today? The question floated in my mind unanswered. I looked around the room. It was so peaceful that I could actually stay in here all day, get some sleep, and watch some TV. Then, I quickly decided against that. Banks had done so much for me in just a few days – the gifts, the space, the dates, the sex. He had given me experiences that I'd never had before, and I wanted to give him the same thing.

So, today, I decided it wasn't going to be about me. I wanted to change it up, do something for him, something thoughtful that he would enjoy. I walked into the closet, eyeing the array of clothes Banks had stocked it with. My fingers skimmed hangers of luxury items with designer tags. I didn't want to look like I was trying too hard, but I also wasn't about to throw on just anything. Banks had a taste for elegance, and I was a reflection of him.

I pulled out a white Fendi crop top, with the classic monogram stitches along the lining in tan, and paired it with light denim jeans by The Row. My sandals and purse were Fendi as well. I placed the gold Cartier jewelry in my ears and around my neck. I moved to the vanity and reached for the matte black bottle, Tom Ford's Fucking Fabulous. I pressed the atomizer several times, allowing the mist to hit my body from different directions.

I loved the scent and was glad that Banks had chosen it. The rich almond and tonka bean smelled amazing on my skin. This was seduction in a bottle, and I thought about wearing it later on tonight. I stared at my reflection for a beat, running a hand through my soft curls that were still intact from the night before. Grabbing my purse, I walked out the room and made my way downstairs.

Just like Zeek had said, the car was parked out front, waiting for me. He opened the car door for me, and I got into the backseat. He handed me Banks' credit card before asking me where we were going. I smiled, more so to myself, as I thought about the lavish, private, at home date night I was about to put together. Banks had been making moves and showing me things I'd never seen. So, tonight was my turn.

"I need to get a few things, so we gon' make a few stops today. First, take me to Saks."

He nodded his head, starting the car, before we pulled down the driveway and out the gate. This would be my first time in Saks Fifth because I'd never had enough money for anything in the store. Now, here I was, about to swipe the black card that Banks had left for me. Zeek pulled up to the door, getting out to open mine. He asked me if I wanted him to go inside with me, but I declined. I didn't want Zeek seeing what I was going inside to buy. He let me know he would be parked in the same spot when I came out, and I nodded before walking inside the building.

The inside of the store was just as beautiful as I had imagined it would be. The dim lighting and cream and gold color scheme looked as elegant as the items sold inside. I walked through the store and over to the lingerie.

A sharply dressed sales associate with red lips and shoulder length, blonde hair approached me. "Are you looking for something in particular?"

I nodded. "Yes. Something so sexy it's going to make my man's mouth drop open the moment he sees me."

The associate didn't flinch. Instead, she smiled knowingly and disappeared into the back. While she was gone, I looked through the shelves and racks for anything I might like. I found a black and white lace panty and bra set that I thought would look amazing on me. I picked it up right before the associate returned holding a garment that damn near took my breath away. It was an emerald green balconette bra with black lace trim, paired with a matching garter belt, and a high cut thong. It was bold but elegant, and I knew it would make a statement when Banks saw me in it.

I walked into the fitting room and tried both pieces on. They both looked good on me, so I decided I would get them both and figure out which one I was going to wear later. I told the associate to box them both up, and I put my clothes back on. When I exited the fitting room, I walked up to the counter and swiped Banks' credit card for my things before walking out of the store.

Just as promised, Zeek was parked right outside where he said he would be, ready to take me to my next stop. I was so excited, and I couldn't wait until I got everything set up. I hoped Banks would like it. He'd shown me so much, and this was only my fourth day here. So, tonight, I was going to switch things up and show him what I could do – the total opposite of everything he was used to. Tonight, I was going to bring him into my world and show him something softer than he'd ever experienced.

Zeek asked me where our next stop was going to be. I told him with a smile before rolling up the partition. About twenty minutes later, we were pulling up to Black Art Materials, an art supply shop that I knew would have everything I needed to make our night perfect. I walked inside the store and was instantly hit with the smell of fresh paint. Every aisle was filled with color, from the paint to the brushes. I took a basket and began shopping.

My first stop was the canvases. I picked up two large ones, as well as two medium sized ones, and placed them inside the basket. Next were the paints. I got every color body paint they had, placing them all into my basket. Then, I went to the brushes and grabbed two sets with different sizes in each. I also grabbed two black linen aprons just in case things got a little messy. In fact, messy was exactly what I wanted to get. I then found two tabletop easels and placed them into the basket as well.

When I stepped up to the counter and placed items on top, the cashier blinked at the pile of supplies.

"You must be having a party."

I smiled. "Yeah, something like that."

She rang me up, and once again, I swiped Banks' card for the items. I walked back to the car, and Zeek put my bags inside. My next stop was the liquor store. We couldn't have a paint and sip without something to sip. I knew Banks did everything big, so I made sure to find one of the most expensive bottles they had in the store, knowing Banks wouldn't have settled for anything less.

After leaving the liquor store, I wasn't done. I still had one more stop to make before it was time for me to go back to the house to set up. I didn't know what time Banks would be back home, but I wanted everything to be perfect when he did. Our last and final stop was to Michael's. This was the exact place I needed to be to create the vibe I wanted.

Knowing I was going to need one, I grabbed a basket the moment I walked inside the store. I walked through the store, looking for the scented candles. I found the aisle and smiled, slowly turning right. I took my time smelling the candles, wanting to put together the perfect scent. I picked thirty candles in different sizes and scents – oud and sandalwood to keep the masculine edge, rose and vanilla to soften it, and amber to bind them all together. I also grabbed several dozen pouches of real dried rose petals, dyed in deep reds and blush pink. I was going to use the rose petals throughout the house, so I made sure to get a lot of them.

After everything was rang up and bagged carefully, I stepped outside where Zeek once again loaded the back of the SUV. When we returned to the estate, Zeek carried all of my bags into the house, placing them gently on the kitchen island.

"You want them all here?" he asked.

"Yeah, this is fine. I can move everything when I set up. Just one more thing, Zeek."

"Sure, what's up?"

"Do you happen to know what time Banks is coming back home?"

"Yeah, I have to go pick him up at eight thirty."

I looked over at the clock. It was already three forty-five. That meant I didn't have much time to set everything up. So, I would have to work fast. I wanted to make this night unforgettable for Banks the way he'd done for me every night since I'd been here.

I stood there for a moment, palms flat on the marble counter, thinking about where I should start. Walking over to the sink, I washed my hands before pulling out everything I would need to make dinner.

With Banks having a private chef, he was sure to keep the kitchen stocked with any and everything. I decided I would start on the crab cakes, putting all the ingredients into a bowl and folding them together before forming the cakes. I placed parchment paper onto a baking sheet and placed the crab cakes on top before placing them into the fridge to set.

I knew they would have to chill for at least thirty minutes, so I took that time to begin setting up. One by one, I carried the bags through the house. I started with the living room, arranging the candles across the fireplace mantle, the coffee table, and the side shelves. I spaced them out to cast soft glows across the room, nothing too bright, just enough to warm the room. Then, I opened one of the bags and let the rose petals slip through my fingers, scattering them across the center of the room and toward the hallway Banks would walk through when he got home.

I moved on to the dining room. The long, mahogany table had already been polished to perfection by the cleaning staff, but I still wiped it down myself, wanting to add a personal touch. I placed tall, narrow candles along the center and surrounded them with rose petals, careful not to overdo it. I didn't want it to look cluttered and tacky but graceful and elegant. I paused and stood back, admiring the blend of firelight and rose petals.

Next, I went back to the kitchen, washed my hands once more, and started to prepare a Caesar salad. I wanted the food to be hot when Banks came home, so cooking would be the last thing I did. With that, I made my way up to my bedroom. I knew this had to be the room that spoke the loudest because this was where we would end the night.

I dimmed the lights and circled the perimeter with oud and vanilla candles. On the bed, I created a trail of rose petals from the steps going up to the pillow. Then, I added a few more on the nightstands and windowsills. Everything looked so nice, and I couldn't wait for Banks to come home. Looking over at the clock that hung on the wall, I saw that it was six o'clock.

I thought for a moment, thinking about where I wanted to set up the paint. I had a few ideas of things I wanted to paint but knew we would need an open space to do it. Walking down the hall, I went to the basement door and walked downstairs. I hadn't been down here since Banks had given me a tour on the first day I got here. There was a large, open space down there that would be perfect for our paint and sip. *Fuck, I need plastic,* I thought to myself.

Walking back upstairs, I went back down the hallway and to the front door. Opening it, I prayed that Zeek was still outside. Thankfully, he was, and he opened the car door the moment he saw me walk out.

"Hey, Braylen. You need something?" he asked as I walked toward him.

"Yes, I do. I need plastic. Thick plastic."

He looked at me skeptically, and I chuckled. "I'm setting up a paint and sip."

"Oh, 'cause a nigga was 'bout to say." He laughed in relief. "Yeah, I can go grab you some. Where do you want me to put it once I bring it back?"

"The basement," I replied, thanking him before walking back into the house.

Walking back upstairs, I went into my room, taking a shower and throwing on a pink yoga set before setting up the bathroom. The only thing I didn't do was run his bath water. That would be something that I waited to do until he was on his way home. I put on my makeup before heading back down to the kitchen to finish cooking. I filled a pot of water and placed it on the stove to boil while I began making the alfredo sauce. Once the water started boiling, I salted it before placing the noodles into the pot.

When the food was ready, I placed it into the oven to keep it warm while I rushed downstairs to set up the basement. I placed the plastic onto the floor before putting the remaining candles and rose petals around the space we would be in. I set the paints, canvases, and brushes onto the table and floor. Once that was done, everything was set, and I headed back to my room.

Opening my nightstand drawer, I grabbed my phone just as it lit up with Vita's name flashing across the screen. I swiped the talk button before placing the phone to my ear.

"Hey, bitch, what's up?" I greeted cheerfully.

"I'm calling to make sure you ain't 'bout to be on the next episode of the *First 48*. And why the fuck do you sound so cheerful in a time like this?"

"Girl, why the hell would I be on that show? And why wouldn't I be cheerful? I have nothing to be sad or mad about."

"Bitch, am I on glue, or did you not tell me that Kyrie sold you to a nigga named Banks? I'm not liking this shit at all, Bray. How many more days of this shit do you have left?"

"It's only Thursday, Vee. I'm here til Monday morning."

"Bitch, how are you okay with this?"

"Vee, have you ever had a nigga bend you over on a yacht and fuck the shit outta you while you overlook the ocean?"

"Bray, you letting that nigga fuck you?"

"No, I'm letting that nigga fuck the shit outta me," I replied.

Vita screamed so loud that I had to pull the phone away from my ear. "Oh, bitch, that's what I'm talkin' 'bout. Fuck Kyrie. Don't ever go back there."

I laughed. Just thirty seconds ago, she was telling me to leave; now she wanted me to stay. Placing the phone on speaker, I placed it on the nightstand, still talking to Vita while I oiled my body and slid into the lingerie I'd purchased earlier. By the time I was dressed, it was exactly eight thirty. I told Vita I would call her tomorrow before placing my phone back into the nightstand and spraying myself from head to toe with Baccarat Rouge 540.

I made my way into the bathroom and ran Banks a hot bubble bath before lighting every candle I'd placed around the house. Once I was done, I made our plates before taking them into the dining room and placing cloches over both plates. I'd just walked into the living room when I saw the headlights coming up the driveway. I quickly rushed back to the kitchen and poured Banks a drink. Grabbing it, I rushed back to the foyer, meeting Banks just as he opened the door.

"Braylen?" Banks said with a smile. I could hear the surprise oozing from his tone. "What the hell is all this?" he asked, looking around at the dim lighting and rose petals on the floor.

I smiled before handing him his drink. Without a word, I grabbed his hand and led him up the stairs. He followed without question, looking down at every rose petal that made a trail throughout the house. We walked inside my room and into the en-suite bathroom where I had a hot bubble bath waiting. I'd placed rose petals inside the water, while I had candles lit all around the tub.

"Take off your clothes," I ordered.

Banks took a sip of his drink and placed his glass onto the counter before he began peeling out of the light gray suit he wore. Banks stood in front of me naked and looking amazing. He stepped down into the bubbly hot water, looking over at me in disbelief. I could tell he was excited about the gesture, and we hadn't even started the date night yet.

He reached up, gently brushing my cheek with the back of his hand. "Damn, you look so good." He licked his lips. "I want to taste that pussy when I get out this tub."

I smiled, walking over to the counter and grabbing his drink, handing it to him. "That's going to have to wait until later. I have plans for us."

"Oh, really? So, what's after this bath?"

"I cooked dinner for us, and it's already in the dining room. I cooked jumbo lump crab cake alfredo, salad, and garlic rolls."

"Damn, that shit sounds good as hell. Let me hurry up and get out this tub."

Banks soaked in the tub for about fifteen minutes until he got into the shower. When he did, I went down and quickly warmed the food up, wanting to make sure it was hot when Bank sat down to eat. I arrived back up just as Banks was putting on the pair of gray sweatpants and black beater I had laid out for him. I licked my lips when I looked at the print of his manhood.

We walked into the dining room; the candles casted a golden haze over the entire room. Bank pulled out my chair for me before taking his seat. He couldn't hide the smile on his face as he looked up at me.

"I can't believe you did all this. Nobody has ever did anything like this for me."

"This is just the beginning. I put together an at home date night for us."

"You what?" Banks chuckled before taking a forkful of pasta into his mouth.

"I planned us a date night. It's my turn to show you something different. So, that's exactly what I'm going to do."

He shook his head in disbelief as he continued to eat. We ate in silence with Banks looking up at me and smiling every so often. Halfway through dinner, he reached across the table and took my hand. "This is nice. Thank you, Braylen."

"I'm glad you like it."

Once dinner was over, I stood to my feet, taking Banks' hand into mine before leading him down to the basement where our paint and sip was set up.

Banks raised a brow when he saw the setup. "You got me paintin' tonight?"

"Yep, we paintin' and sippin' tonight." I walked over to the table and poured two glasses of the expensive liquor before handing one to Banks. We toasted before taking sips. Banks told me about the hidden speakers in the celling and offered to turn on some music. I agreed, and he chose soft R&B to match the vibe I'd already set.

We squeezed the different colors of paint onto palettes before opening all the brushes. I used to love to paint and was very good at it. However, this was something else I'd stopped doing after getting married to Kyrie. With his gambling addiction, I never had the money to restock any of my paint supplies. And most of the ones I did have, Kyrie had sold when he needed money to gamble away at the casino.

We started at the table, painting on the medium sized canvases. At first, Banks looked very focused, with his tongue slightly poking from the corner of his mouth and his eyes narrowed as he ran his brush across the canvas. That was until I looked over at him and busted out laughing, looking at the stick figure he was painting.

"Oh, you laughing at my painting? And before you answer, keep in mind that I'm an artist, and I'm sensitive about my shit."

I couldn't help it. I was laughing so hard I could barely breathe as tears ran from my eyes. "Nigga, who is you? Last name Badu, first name Erykah?"

"Oh, you talkin' big shit. Well, you just wait until I add my sunny sky and flying birds. I bet you won't be laughing at my masterpiece then."

We both laughed as we continued to sip and paint. About an hour later, we were done, and just as promised, Banks had added a sunny sky and birds to the two stick figures he'd painted. When he looked at my painting, his mouth dropped open. It was a picture of the ocean and the starry sky with the yacht we were on the night before.

"Braylen, you can really paint? This is really good."

"Yeah, I used to paint a lot, then I stopped. But I still love it."

"You should start back painting. This is a gift that you can't waste." He grabbed my chin, looking me directly in the eye. "Always chase your dreams. If you gon' bet on anything, put that shit on yourself."

I smiled, nodding my head before pouring us both another drink. He told me he was going to get both of the pictures framed and was going to hang them up somewhere in the house. The look on his face let me know he was serious, so I didn't do anything but nod my head.

"We're not done yet." I downed my drink before placing the glass back on the table. "Take off your clothes."

He looked at me with a smile but didn't protest. He pulled off his sweatpants and beater, and I poured different colors of paint into plastic red cups I'd placed on the side of the table. Once I was finished, I took off the lingerie I had on.

"Damn, I was hoping I was going to take that off of you," Banks spoke as he walked closer to me.

"Don't worry. What I have planned next is going to be ten times better than you just simply removing a pair of panties and a bra." I picked up a few cups from the table. "Can you help me bring the rest of these over to the plastic?"

Banks grabbed the rest of the cups, walking them over and setting them onto the floor. He didn't say a word, just watched me for the next move. Slowly, I walked back over to the table, being sure to make my ass jiggle as I walked. Bending over and picking up the bag of large paint brushes, I gave Banks a full view of my pretty pussy. I wanted to put on a show. Pouring two more drinks, I turned around to see Banks' manhood standing at attention. I smiled, knowing my little show had worked.

Walking back over to him, I handed him his glass before taking the paint brushes from the bag. I handed two to him, while I kept the other two. Sipping from my drink, I eyed Banks.

"We're about to paint each other," I finally spoke, placing my drink onto the table.

Banks rose his brow before cracking a smile. I walked over to the cups, grabbing the dark blue paint. Dipping my brush inside, I walked over to Banks. I ran the brush over a portion of his neck before trailing the blue paint down the front of his chest. Then, I grabbed a deep purple and did the same thing. After that came green and then black, every color as bold as Banks' personality. I asked him to lay on the canvas on the floor. He did so, and I laid on top of him, lightly pressing him to the canvas.

When I was done, we both stood to our feet. He did the same, grabbing the cups and painting down my body. Banks used bright colors – yellow, pink, orange, and white – before I laid down on the canvas. He laid on top of me, just as I had done him, his body heat feeling good against my skin. When he got up, so did I, and I looked down at my body on the canvas.

I let Banks know we needed to allow the paintings twelve hours to fully dry before we could move them. I walked back over to the table and grabbed the liquor bottle and my cup before motioning for Banks to follow me. Grabbing his glass, he allowed me to lead him back up to my bedroom where we would finish off the night.

We walked into the room, paint all over us, and walked directly into the bathroom. I placed the bottle onto the counter before turning on the shower. We both finished the rest of the liquor in our glasses before getting into the shower. The hot water ran down our bodies, washing the paint away. I lathered the loofah before washing every inch of Banks' body, and then he did the same to mine.

This was the softest Banks had been with me since I'd arrived here, and I welcomed the change. He pulled me into him, placing his hand under my chin and guiding my lips toward his. He kissed me so deeply and passionately that my knees buckled. We stayed in the shower, allowing the water to run down our bodies, for several moments, allowing our tongues to dance as we became lost in one another.

Once out the shower, I handed Banks a towel before wrapping another one over my wet body. He poured more liquor into our glasses. By this point, the liquor had me feeling good, and I knew Banks was too. We walked out of the bathroom and into the bedroom area. I walked over to the bed where I'd placed rose petals all over. I was just about to take a seat when Banks stopped me, pulling me to him and kissing me once more. I allowed him to kiss me because I knew that after this, I would be in control of everything else for the rest of the night.

I ran my fingers down the center of his chest. "Sit down," I whispered.

He obeyed, taking a seat on the edge of the bed. I stepped up onto the bed, climbed into his lap, and straddled him. I rolled my hips slow, teasing him, allowing him to feel the wetness coming from between my legs without even being inside of me.

His voice was low. "Braylen..."

I placed my finger to his lips, stopping him, before he said another word. "Let me," I whispered.

I kissed his jaw softly before making my way to his neck. "You always take care of me. Tonight, I want to take care of you."

He didn't argue, just allowed me to place a trail of kisses from his neck to his chest. I took my time with him. My fingers traced the lines of his tattoos slowly. I bit his shoulder gently and felt him exhale slowly.

"Lay back," I ordered.

He moved back on the bed, head hitting the pillows, body stretched out long across the mattress. I was still on top of him, our eyes locked together. Slowly, I slid my towel off my body, throwing it to the floor. I leaned down, kissing him deeply on the lips, our tongues locking and twirling between one another's. His hands gripped my thighs but didn't guide me. He let me ride the pace, let me tease him as I rocked to a beat that we both understood. I ran my warm wetness over his manhood without letting it slip inside of me.

I scooted down and rested between his legs. Wrapping my hand around his thick manhood, I spit on his head before taking him into my mouth. I watched as his fists balled into the sheets as he bit his bottom lip.

"Fuck, Braylen," he moaned.

I kept going, taking him deeper into my mouth. Moving faster, I swirled my tongue around his tip. His hips tightened, hands tangling in my hair. I let him guide me for a moment, let him lose control at how fast or slow I moved my mouth. No matter what he did or how he moved my head, I never stopped sucking.

I felt the head of his dick begin to swell, and I knew he was about to cum. Not wanting him to, I stopped before looking into his eyes. "You bet not cum yet."

He nodded in understanding, still biting his bottom lip.

I straddled him once more. This time, I sank down onto him slowly, letting every inch of him stretch me open. My head fell back from the pressure as he filled me.

"Shit," he breathed.

"Be still for me," I whispered.

I could feel him underneath me, trying not to move as I rode him in slow circles. I watched as he tilted his head back before rolling his eyes into the back of his head.

"Yeah, baby, just like that," he moaned.

The room filled with the sounds of our bodies moving together as I bounced up and down on his manhood. I rode him harder now, my nails dragging down his chest as I leaned forward, kissing him, tasting his tongue while I moved my hips with precision. He reached up, pinching one of my nipples, and I gasped, grinding down harder in response.

"You tryna make me cum before you do?" he whispered.

"Just hold it."

He flipped us suddenly, gripping my wrists and pinning them above my head. Now, he was on top, inside me deep, with slow strokes.

"I let you have your fun," he said with a wicked smirk. "Now, it's my turn."

He thrust hard and deep. I arched my back, opening my legs wider.

"Banks!"

"Yeah, that's right, baby. Say that shit again," he demanded, slamming into me.

"Banks! Yes, baby. Fuck me!"

He bit my neck, dragged his teeth across my collarbone, and drove into me like he was claiming me from the inside out. My orgasm hit like fire through my veins, my whole body convulsing under him as I cried out his name. But he didn't stop. He wasn't done.

He flipped me onto my stomach and pulled my hips up, entering me from behind, this time slower and deeper.

"This pussy's mine now," he moaned against my ear.

"Yes, Daddy. This pussy all yours," I panted, gripping the sheets.

He wrapped his hand around my throat, holding onto me just enough to let me know who I belonged to. My second orgasm built even quicker this time, causing me to tremble underneath him.

Banks slowly pulled out of me before sitting up. Before he could do anything else, I leaned up, taking him inside my mouth once more, being sure to lick all my juices from his shaft. He moaned, grabbing my head before leaning forward and smacking my ass. His entire body jerked as the slurping noises filled the room.

"Fuck," he moaned out as he gripped a handful of my ass.

I took him deeper, faster, gagging slightly and moaning while I sucked. Slowly pulling him from my mouth, I stroked him while I licked both of his balls, taking them both into my mouth and sucking softly.

Sitting back up, I ordered Banks to lay back down, and he did so without a word. I climbed back over him and sat on his face. He groaned as I lowered myself, and when his tongue met my center, I damn near collapsed.

"Fuckkkk, Banks!"

He gripped my thighs tight and pulled me down harder against his mouth, devouring me like he was starving. I rode his face, my hips moving in slow circles. I looked down and watched his eyes staring up at me. My body trembled. I was cumming again. I held onto the headboard as my orgasm rolled through me, my legs shaking uncontrollably.

He moaned softly from between my legs, his tongue still moving in circles around my clit. His fingers slid inside me while he continued to lick.

I fell off him with a gasp, my body completely drained, but he wasn't done. He flipped me onto my stomach and slid inside me from behind again, this time holding both my wrists behind my back with one hand while he fucked me deep. His strokes were slow and long, and I felt every inch of him.

I looked back at him, eyes glassy. "Harder," I spoke. He blinked like he couldn't believe what I just said. I pushed up on my elbows, arching my back more. "You heard me. I said do it harder."

He gripped my hips and slammed into me, each thrust stealing the air from my lungs.

He pulled out suddenly and flipped me over. "Put your legs up."

I obeyed. He slid back in with my legs on his shoulders, the angle hitting a spot so deep I screamed.

"Banks!"

"Yeah, that's right, baby. This pussy mine. You made her cum for me, now make her squirt for me."

He leaned down and sucked one of my nipples, fingers playing with the other while he kept stroking me from the inside. His hips didn't slow. Neither did the wet slapping sounds that echoed off the bedroom walls. He pulled out again and dragged me down to the edge of the bed. "Open your mouth."

I did as I was told, opening my mouth wide. He slid himself inside, groaning as I sucked him with my eyes locked on his. I moaned as I sucked. He pulled out and lifted me off the bed, carrying me over to the wall like I weighed nothing. He slammed me up against it, lifted one of my thighs, and pushed inside me again. We were face to face now, sweaty and panting.

"I ever tell you how good your pussy feels?" he rasped.

"Tell me, baby."

He kissed me, fucking me harder. The wall behind me vibrated from the force. His sweat dripped down my back, and my fingers glided across his skin. I bit down on his shoulder, and he snapped. He carried me back to the bed and put me on my back before spreading my legs wide. He fingered me fast, not stopping until I squirted. I gasped, not even knowing that was something I could do. My legs were shaking, and my thighs were soaked.

He slid back in before I could even recover, stroking that same spot, pulling moans out of me like he knew my body better than I did.

"You wanted to take it there," he whispered. "So don't run now."

"I'm not," I gasped.

He crawled on top of me, sliding into my wetness with ease. He stroked and moaned into my ear. "I'm gonna cum," he whispered.

I kissed him. "Do it."

We stared into each other's eyes as he came, moaning into my mouth, his entire body tensing on top of mine.

When it was over, we didn't move. We laid there, tangled between one another. He kissed my temple as he rested on top of me. He could have stayed right there forever. I didn't want him to move because I loved the way his body felt on mine.

I thought we were done. I really did. However, then he rolled me over onto my side and slid inside me again, so slow, so deep, I almost cried.

"Just one more," he whispered into the crook of my neck. "I need to feel you again."

I whimpered, already sensitive beyond belief, but I didn't stop him. I couldn't. There was no force in his movements this time, just ease. His hand slid under my thigh, lifting it slightly for better access, and I let my eyes close, my lips parting on a breathless moan.

"God, you feel like Heaven," he murmured, kissing my shoulder.

I arched into him, pressing my back tighter against his chest. The stretch felt too good. My body molded to his rhythm naturally, hips moving with his in sync like we were made for this. For each other.

His lips stayed on my skin, kissing me slow as his fingers slid between my legs and found my clit again. I gasped. I twisted my neck and caught his mouth in a kiss, our tongues tangled in slow movements.

Our movements got faster. I came first, biting into his bottom lip as I clenched around him, my orgasm crashing over me like a wave I couldn't fight. Banks' followed, pulsing inside me with a groan so low it vibrated against my back. He held me like that, buried deep, arms wrapped tight around my waist, as he caught his breath. We didn't speak for a while. The room was quiet except for our breathing.

Finally, he pulled out and rolled onto his back, dragging me with him so that I was lying half on his chest, half on the bed. His arm stayed looped around my waist, his fingers tracing lazy circles on my bare hip.

"You good?" he asked softly.

I nodded against his chest. "Yeah. You?"

A low laugh rumbled from his chest. "I'm better than good."

I smiled. My whole body felt like it had melted, like there wasn't a single bone left in me. Everything ached in the best possible way. He kissed the top of my head then looked down at me.

"I don't think I want to go back to my room tonight. I don't even want to leave you," he confessed.

I lifted my head a little, surprised. "You don't?"

He had never said this before. Any other time we fucked, no matter how good it was, Banks always left after, without even saying a word. Now, here he was, telling me that he didn't want to leave me.

He shook his head. "Nah. I want to stay right here with you."

I blinked. We'd done everything else. Sex, meals, and dates. But sleep together was something we'd never done. The truth was that I didn't want him to leave either.

"Okay," I said, settling back down against him.

His arm tightened around me. I closed my eyes and pressed my cheek against his chest.

He pulled the covers over us and adjusted the pillows, making sure I was tucked in before dimming the bedside lamp. The room darkened to a soft glow, just enough moonlight spilling through the window to cast a sliver glow over the room. His body was warm against mine, solid and protective. I could feel his heart beating, and when I closed my eyes and listened to the rhythm of my own heartbeat, I realized they matched. We fell asleep in each other's arms, and in that moment, I felt like there was nowhere else in the world that I would rather be.

Chapter Fourteen

BANKS

Braylen was still sleeping when I woke up. Her bare shoulder peeked out from under the sheets, caramel skin glowing softly in the morning light that filtered through the curtains. My arm had been draped over her waist all night, and I hadn't moved once. For the first time in a long time, sleep came easy. I shifted just enough to prop my head on my hand and just looked at her.

The night she planned for me was the most amazing night I'd had in a very long time. Every detail was planned out perfectly, and I could tell that she'd put a lot of thought into it. It was intimate, and I knew that a woman wouldn't just do that for any man – only for someone she truly cared about. Was she truly starting to develop feeling for me? My feelings for her came the moment I felt the warmth of her pussy, but last night took things to a different level. There was no lust in the room last night. What I felt was much deeper than that.

This shit really had me wondering if I ha d made love for the first time last night. In all of my twenty-six years, I'd never made love. However, after last night, I felt like I had. My fingers brushed a strand of hair off her cheek, and I leaned in, lips hovering close enough to feel her breath against mine. I didn't kiss her because I didn't want to wake her. I just needed to be close to her.

I climbed out the bed as quietly as I could, wrapping a towel around my waist as I left her room and made my way to mine. There was something I needed to do for her now. I wanted to give her something small in return to start our day right. She gave me a memory last night that I would never forget. So, I wanted to do the same for her. Grabbing my phone from my pants pocket, I placed a call to Marcus.

"What up doe?" his groggy voice answered.

"You up?" I asked.

"Now I am. What's up?"

"I need you to make a breakfast, something good. Not just bacon and eggs. I need something nice for Braylen."

"I got you. Give me thirty," he said before hanging up.

I showered in silence. The hot water ran down my body as I thought about the way Braylen had taken the lead last night. The way she touched me and the way she looked at me felt different from anyone else. She didn't seem scared to be here anymore. To me, she felt comfortable, and it was natural. She wanted to explore me, and I let her. That was foreign to me. I had never trusted a woman enough to fully let myself go and allow her to lead during sex. I was always in control. But last night, Braylen was, and it felt good.

After my shower, I dressed in a fresh pair of gray sweatpants and a white tee. I put on a crisp pair of socks and slid into my Gucci slides before making my way down to the kitchen. When I arrived, I saw that Marcus had already plated food and placed it on a tray.

"I went all out," he said. "Cheesecake stuffed French toast with caramel drizzle and pecans. Scrambled eggs, turkey bacon, hash browns, and fresh fruit on the side. I also made mimosas with just a splash of champagne."

I nodded, appreciating the effort. "Thank you, Marcus."

He had arranged everything on a silver tray, adding a single white rose in a narrow glass vase. Two folded white linen napkins set next to the utensils. I picked it up and walked back up to Braylen's room. She was stirring in bed when I entered. She rolled over, reaching over to the other side of the bed. She opened her eyes when she didn't feel me there.

"Good morning." I smiled.

She rubbed her eyes and smiled back at me, voice still heavy with sleep. "Hey."

"I brought us a little something," I said, walking over and setting the tray onto the bed beside her.

Her eyes widened as she looked down at it. "Banks, you didn't..."

"You gave me something last night. I just wanted to return the gesture. This is nothing, just the start of what is going to be a beautiful day."

She looked up at me with that same fire in her eyes from last night, but this time, it was softer. I sat beside her as she took the first bite of the French toast, moaning low and nodding.

"Okay," she said with a grin. "You're tryin' to spoil me I see."

I tilted my head. "Tryin'?"

She laughed, picked up her mimosa, then I picked up mine. We toasted to a beautiful day together before both taking sips from the glass. I watched as she cut into her French toast once more before placing it into her mouth. Closing her eyes, she slid the food from the fork.

"This is really good," she spoke.

"I figured you deserved something nice after what you gave me last night."

She glanced at me over her glass. "So, you liked it?"

"I didn't just like it," I assured, placing a forkful of eggs into my mouth. "I needed it."

Her eyes softened as she looked at me. That was the truth; I needed last night. Not just the sex. Not just her body. I needed someone to see me, to do something for me without expecting anything in return – someone to put in effort – and that was exactly what Braylen had done.

When we finished eating, I set the tray on the nightstand and laid back beside her. She rested her head on my chest, and I ran my fingers through her hair. We stayed like that for a while, not speaking. She didn't have to because we both knew what it was.

Several moments later, she looked up at me before she whispered, "Thank you."

I kissed the top of her head. "You don't gotta thank me, baby."

"So," she started, looking up at me with that smile that made me want to give her anything she asked for, "how are we spending the rest of the day?"

I took a sip of my mimosa and looked at her over the rim of the glass. "Thought maybe I'd let you take the lead again. You been on a roll lately."

She blushed, laughing lightly, and nudged me with her foot. "Nah, your turn. I done set the bar too high."

I set the glass down and turned to face her more. "Alright. What if we keep it simple today? Hit the garden. Walk the trail behind the house. Maybe spend some time at the outdoor pool. I can even call my massage tech over and give us a couple's massage if you want to."

Her eyes lit up. "That sounds perfect." She leaned in, brushing her lips against mine as she kissed me softly.

"I'm gonna go get this tray outta here," I said, standing and lifting the breakfast tray from the nightstand. "I'll be right back."

I left her room and made my way down the stairs, heading into the kitchen where Marcus was already cleaning up. I set the tray on the counter and gave him a nod. Before I could turn to go back upstairs, the doorbell chimed. I frowned, not knowing who was at my door. Nobody came to my door without clearance – not unless they were suicidal. Zeek hadn't texted me nor had the cameras pinged. I walked toward the door, barefoot, jaw already tightening. When I opened it, my mood dropped instantly.

Standing there, looking like he hadn't slept in days, was Kyrie. His eyes met mine, bloodshot but steady. He didn't speak right away.

My voice came out low and sharp. "You got about five seconds to explain what the fuck you doing at my door."

Kyrie didn't flinch. He stepped forward and pulled a duffle bag from his shoulder. He opened it, showing me the cash that was inside, neatly wrapped in bundles.

"It's all here, a hundred bands," he said, lifting the bag slightly. "Every penny of what I owe you. You can count it up if you want to." He kept going, like he'd practiced this shit in the mirror. "I'm here to get my wife."

I didn't say shit. The world just slowed. I saw his chest rise like he was proud of himself, while all I felt was anger boiling in my veins.

"You really dumb enough to come to my house with a bag full of money and a request like that?" I asked, stepping onto the porch now, toe to toe with him.

"She don't belong here," he said. "Whatever y'all been doing, it's over now. I'm square with you. Let her go."

Let her go? He said the words like she was a prisoner or some shit. Like I hadn't just spent the night with her wrapped around me, whispering my name, moaning like I was the only man to ever touch her soul. I laughed because he clearly had me fucked up.

"You think she ain't here by choice?" I asked, voice low. "You think I forced her to stay with me?"

His jaw flexed. "Nah, you trying to get in her head, but that shit ain't gone work. I'm here now, and I'm comin' to get my wife."

"You mean the wife I treated better in four days than you did in five years? Nigga, don't forget the only reason she's here is because you gave her to me. Yo bum ass wanted to gamble so bad that you would hand over yo queen to do so."

"Is that why you been texting me from her phone, trying to act like you're her?"

"Nigga, what? Don't ever insult me like that. I'm a grown ass man and would never do nothing so childish." I was pissed, both at the fact that Braylen had spoken to him after I'd told her not to and at the fact he thought I would ever text him from someone else's phone like some bitch ass nigga.

His hand twitched, and I took a step closer and welcomed him. Kyrie knew how I got down. He was standing in front of me with only nine fingers because of it. If he wanted to leave here missing eight more, I was fine with that.

"I gave you what you wanted," he snapped. "The money. That was the deal. Now give me back my fucking wife."

"That was your debt," I snapped back. "Not a fuckin' trade." I stared at him. "You don't own her. And I damn sure ain't about to give her to a man who sold her in the first place."

He dropped the duffle bag to the ground with a hard thud. "You don't know shit about what I've been through to get that money."

"Nor do I give a fuck. I'm not impressed. You should've been working this hard to be the man she needed *before* you handed her over like a fuckin' pawn."

Kyrie looked past me like he was searching for a glimpse of her through the front windows. That pissed me off more than anything.

"She ain't yours anymore. And the next time you show up at my door like this, I promise you won't leave."

"I'll let her decide that," he muttered. "She still my wife."

I stepped in front of him again. "In case you didn't know, she already decided. She upstairs gettin' that pussy wet for me right now. If she chooses to come back to you Monday morning, then that's when she will be back. Now take yo little money cause this ain't shit to me." I kicked the duffle bag back over to him.

He looked like he wanted to say something else – chest rising and falling, mouth parting – but no words left his lips. I stepped back inside and slammed the door shut. I locked it before turning around and walking back upstairs. My blood boiled as I clenched my fists tightly. I should have killed him, dropped him right then and there for his disrespect. However, I knew Braylen would never talk to me again if I did that. She was the only thing that saved his life, and I hoped he knew that. If he ever brought his ass back to my home, I couldn't promise that it would end the same way.

"You good?" Braylen asked, seeing the look on my face when I walked inside her bedroom.

"Your husband was just at my door, trying to give me the money he owed me. He said he was here to get you."

"What? Kyrie was here?" she asked in surprise.

"That was exactly how I felt when I opened my door and saw him standing there. I wondered how he'd gotten my address. Then, he told me that he'd talked to you. Well, actually, he thought it was me texting him from your phone. I thought that was crazy because I'd already told you not to talk to him while you were in my house."

"What? I haven't talked to him since I been here. There was no need for me to say shit to him."

"Then why the fuck would he say that?"

She paused for a moment as if she was thinking. "He must have my location or something, Banks, because I didn't give him your address. And I haven't spoken with him at all." She paused again. "Wait, the other night, I texted him and told him to stop calling and texting me. But we didn't talk. That was all I said. He had been texting and calling me nonstop, and I was tired of it. But that was all I sent."

"Do you want to go back to that nigga?"

Her mouth dropped. "What?"

"You heard me," I snapped. "You want to go back to the nigga that gave you to me in the first place? That used you to wipe his debt clean. Is that what you want to go back to?"

"I *don't* want to go back," she spoke. "If I wanted to be there, I would have never came here in the first place. I'm trying to show you that I care about you because I do." Tears began to fall from her eyes. "I'm supposed to be here until Monday, and it's only Friday. Do you want me to go?"

"Hell no! I want you to stay with me, but I need to be sure that's what you want to do."

She walked up closer to me, wrapped her arms around me, and placed her head on my chest. "I want to stay here with you. Let's not let him ruin the day we were planning to have. That's all he ever wants to do – ruin shit."

I nodded my head before kissing her on the top of hers. Braylen was right. Before that nigga had shown up unannounced, we were about to plan another perfect day together. There was no way I was going to allow him – or anyone else – to ruin that.

Chapter Fifteen

KYRIE

The drive back to my townhouse was a blur. I couldn't focus on the road – or on anything else for that matter. My hands gripped the steering wheel tightly. Every inch of me felt tense – like I was holding onto a rope that was about to snap. I couldn't believe this shit was really happening.

I walked up to Banks' door, handed him the money, and still, he didn't give me my fucking wife back. What the fuck was he doing? The only reason she was even there was because he wanted his hundred racks. I had given it to him, yet he still wanted to keep her. Was he keeping her there against her will? Or did she truly want to be there?

I needed to see her, to talk to her. There was no way the Braylen I knew would leave me for anyone. She was the most loyal woman I'd ever met. I knew she wasn't supposed to return until Monday, but damn. I had the fucking money, so what else did he want? Braylen was my wife, and no other man was going to keep her from me.

I clenched my jaw so tight it hurt. Did this nigga really think he was going to take my wife from me? He must have forgot she's only there because I told her to go. Him telling me that I couldn't get my fucking wife back was what I wasn't fuckin' with. He was over there, buying bitches to fuck with, and had the nerve to tell me who I wasn't taking? That nigga used to put fear in my heart, and now, this muthafucka had quickly turned into the weakest nigga I knew. Buying pussy to fall in love with. That nigga was going to have to try that shit with somebody else because he wasn't taking my wife.

I thought I had a plan. This shit was supposed to be easy. The hardest part should have been getting the money. Did he even want the money? Had all this been a setup just so he could get my wife? I refused to believe that Braylen didn't want to come back home. Banks was forcing her to stay, and I had to figure out a way to get her back. I slammed my hand against the steering wheel as I made a sharp turn into my townhome.

I parked the car before walking inside. The silence was loud as hell, and I knew I wouldn't have peace until Braylen was back home where she belonged. It felt like everything I had done to try to win her back had fallen apart in that one moment. I should've been stronger and never sent her over there in the first place. I had the fucking money, and if I had never gotten jumped that morning, none of this would have happened.

No matter what happened over the years, I loved Braylen more than anything. The only reason she was even over there was because she loved me too. She loved me so much that she was willing to do anything I needed her to do to save my life. Once you loved a nigga the way Braylen loved me, no other nigga would be able to take her. Banks could try all he wanted, but I knew my baby, and there was no way she would not be home by Monday.

I tried to calm down knowing that. If there was one thing I knew, Banks was a man of his word. So, I knew when the agreement we had was over, she would be returned. I just thought he would want the money more. I guess I was wrong. The question was could I wait until Monday?

My mind was racing, and I was all over the place. I needed to clear my head so that I could think. I walked up to my room, placing the bag of money that Banks didn't want into my closet. Taking off my clothes, I tossed my suit across the chair in my room and went to take a shower. I'd been up all night, trying to get the money to get Braylen back. My head felt heavy, and my eyes burned. I quickly washed my body before getting out the shower.

I needed rest. My body felt like I'd gone ten rounds in the ring with the heavyweight champion of the world, and my mind was even worse. I laid down in bed, naked, not caring enough to put anything on. I stared up at the ceiling until my eyes shut.

I woke up hours later. Rolling over, I looked at the clock on my nightstand. It was six forty-five in the evening. I had a little over two hours before I needed to be at the warehouse to meet with Vic and the crew. I sat up slowly, still groggy but a little clearer than I had been earlier. That nap had been like a reset button.

I knew we were going to hit another casino tonight, and yesterday, Vic told me that I needed to look the part. The only suit I had was the one that Vic had gotten me, and I knew I couldn't wear that same one again. So, with that, I got dressed in my same jeans that I wore every day and a fresh white tee. I changed my bandage before putting on my shoes. I counted out twenty thousand in cash from the money in the duffle bag.

I didn't know much about suits, but I knew that everyone with money talked about Saks Fifth, so that was where I went. I didn't have much time, so I walked in and asked the first associate I saw to point me in the direction of the suits. I'd looked at the size of the one Vic got me, so I knew exactly what I was looking for. She showed me to the suits, and I picked out three. Then, I went over to the shirts and picked out three of those. Next, the shoes. I picked out one pair, and I was ready to go. Five thousand dollars later, I was walking back out to my car.

By the time I pulled up at the warehouse, the sun was setting, casting a deep orange glow over the sky. Popping my trunk, I grabbed one of the suits, a shirt, and the shoes I'd just purchased and headed up to the door. Vic was already watching the parking lot because the moment I walked up to the door, it opened. I walked in, speaking to everyone, before walking to the bathroom. Ten minutes later, I was dressed and walking back out.

We didn't waste any time, getting right down to business. After a short rundown from Vic, we all loaded up and headed to the MGM Grand downtown. The closer we got, the more my mind sharpened, locking into that zone and getting into the game.

The crew walked in like strangers, not even making eye contact with one another. We split up as soon as we passed through the security check. I made my way to a Blackjack table near the high-roller section. I had on my fresh black suit I'd just purchased, and it fit like it was made for me. I looked like I belonged at the table – no matter how much the bets were. The dealer was some older, white man with hair that was turning slightly gray.

Tasha sat across the floor, a few tables down. She was playing distraction, sitting at the table, making conversation with some rich man, laughing at all his corny jokes. Simone moved through the casino like the wind, hovering between tables like she couldn't decide where she wanted to play, while Vic was already deep into a game near the back, casually winning.

I tracked the count in my head. I kept it running silently in my mind like a second heartbeat. At first, I played low with fifty-dollar bets. The moment the count swung heavy in our favor, I upped my bet to five hundred dollars. I doubled down on an eleven, and the dealer dealt me a ten – blackjack. Simone caught my eye from across the room and gave the signal, a slight tug of her long, gold earring. She'd been watching tables and knew it was time to rotate. I stood to my feet, gathered my chips like I was bored, and wandered over to the next table.

We did this for hours – moving from table to table, playing hand after hand. The count shifted like waves, and we rode it like professionals. We never stayed too long at the same table, rotating every hour. At one point, a security guy started making his way toward Vic. I was on high alert the moment I saw it, but Vic handled it smoothly. He stood up with a grin and pointed at the bar like he was headed for a drink. He left the chips, grabbed his phone, and disappeared into the crowd. Ten minutes later, he sat at another table with Simone and ordered whiskey like nothing happened.

By two in the morning, we were all back in the truck. Back at the warehouse, nobody said much until we locked the doors behind us. Tasha dropped her purse on the table and pulled out the black, leather bag where we'd stashed all the money. Vic broke out the money counter and began running the money through.

"Three hundred seventy-eight thousand, six hundred dollars."

My mouth went dry, not believing the amount of money we'd just made. Tasha laughed, and Simone let out a whistle. We split the money four ways. That meant ninety-four thousand, six hundred and fifty dollar each – all in one night. I nodded to myself, proud of my night's work. Vic told me we would be going to Motor City Casino tomorrow night, and I was ready. Grabbing my money, I walked out the warehouse and headed to my car.

I pulled up to the house just before three in the morning. I couldn't wait for Braylen to come home and see all the money I'd been making. I had almost a hundred thousand dollars, and that was all in one night. If I continued to do this, I would be rich in just a few short weeks.

I dropped the money on the kitchen table and stood there in the dark for a minute, my hands gripping the edge of the table. My head hung low, wishing Braylen was here. Walking into the kitchen, I turned on the light before making myself a turkey sandwich. Bringing my plate to the dining room table along with a bottle of water, I sat down to eat. When I was done, I washed my plate and grabbed my money before heading up to my room. I tucked the money away in the closet along with the rest of the money I'd made. I took off my suit before remembering the others I'd bought were still in the car.

Opting to grab them in the morning, I walked into the bathroom and got into the shower. When I got out, I changed my bandage before heading back to my room. I was so tired that I could hardly see straight. My eyes closed the moment my head hit the pillow, and I drifted off to sleep.

Chapter Sixteen

BRAYLEN

The water was hot as it ran down my body. I stood under the stream in silence, my palms flat against the shower tile. My head was down, and my eyes were closed. All I could think about was Kyrie showing up. What the fuck was he thinking? He showed up here out the blue and with money, the full amount. A hundred fucking thousand dollars. Where the hell did he get that amount of money from?

My mind ran in circles, trying to make it make sense. Kyrie didn't have money like that. That muthafucka didn't have money at all. The little bit he did have at times was quickly gambled away the moment it hit his pocket. The last time I checked, we were scraping together rent and arguing over grocery lists. Now, suddenly, he had six figures in cash? Hell no. I could only wonder what he'd gotten himself into this time to have that type of cash on hand.

I opened my eyes slowly, watching the water bead down my arms and my thighs. The steam curled around me like smoke. Was he selling something? Did he rob somebody? So many thoughts ran through my mind, and no matter how much I tried to get Kyrie out of my head, I couldn't.

Kyrie wasn't no damn kingpin, so I hoped he hadn't resorted to selling any type of drugs. He wasn't built for that kind of life, no matter what he thought. So, if he really had come up with that kind of money, I knew he had to be doing something reckless, something that would probably cause more harm than he'd already caused. What the hell did he think was going to happen? That he'd show up, throw some money down like he was cashing out a damn receipt, and I'd just run back to him like nothing happened? He had to be out his fucking mind if he thought that was going to happen. I took a deep breath and turned around, letting the water hit my back now.

I hoped Banks believed me when I said I hadn't given Kyrie his address or even talked to him. I'd forgotten all about Kyrie having my location. I would have turned that shit off the moment I left the house if I did. Banks hadn't said much since telling me Kyrie came by. However, I could feel the tension radiating off him like heat. So, I knew he was upset. I couldn't blame him though because I would be too.

I wasn't dumb. I knew what kind of man Banks was, and I knew his name carried weight. I didn't know how much weight nor what kind, but I knew his name rang bells in the streets. I knew his hands were nowhere near clean, but I didn't care. Nobody made me feel the way Banks made me feel. Not even my husband. I felt safer with Banks than I'd ever felt in my life.

I'd only been here for a few days, but somehow, he'd managed to undo knots I didn't even know I was carrying. He'd peeled back parts of me I thought I'd buried for good. The woman Kyrie had forced me to be, the woman that I didn't like when I looked at myself in the mirror, was slowly starting to leave, while the woman I used to be was coming back – the woman I loved being before I was Kyrie's wife. Banks saw me for the woman I was supposed to be and not for who someone told me I should be.

I'd loved Kyrie so much that I was willing to change who I was to please him. Meanwhile, he was continuously taking and taking from me without pouring anything back into me. I just couldn't take that anymore. However, Kyrie was still my husband. I was so torn, and it was all Kyrie's fault. If he would have never made me come here, none of this would be happening.

I finally reached for the soap and started washing my body. I scrubbed slowly, trying to wash off the confusion and anger that I felt. On the other hand, I also felt guilt. Here I was, a married woman ready to risk it all. Was I wrong? Was my husband even worth me calling him my husband anymore? Being here with Banks had shown me that I deserved better than what Kyrie had given me.

How could Kyrie ever tell me he loved me again after he'd used me as collateral? Waking up next to Kyrie was like waking up next to silence where love should've been. However, waking up next to Banks was like a new adventure every day. New experiences, new love, and new happiness. Could I give all that up and go back to being unhappy?

The water started to get cold, snapping me out of my thoughts. I turned the water off and stood there a moment longer before stepping out, wrapping myself in a thick white towel. My reflection stared back at me in the mirror, damp curls clinging to my body. I stepped up closer to the mirror, really looking at myself. For the first time in a long time, I didn't look sad. When I smiled, it wasn't forced, and I knew that it was because of Banks.

I walked out the bathroom and looked around, but Banks wasn't in the room. I hoped he was somewhere calming down. I hoped he could allow this moment to pass instead of turning it into something we couldn't come back from. I didn't want to fight with him. I wanted to have fun with him. I wanted to move past this and have a beautiful day together like we'd planned. I hoped he wanted the same.

I got dressed, hoping the day could still be salvaged. The energy between Banks and me had shifted, and I could feel the tension hanging in the air. Last night was perfect and so was this morning. I hoped the rest of our day could be just as perfect. There was a quiet tension hanging in the air, but I didn't want to lose the softness we had built the past few days.

I stepped into a breezy, cream-colored Saint Laurent sundress with thin straps and a high slit on one side. It felt light – exactly like how I wanted today to feel. I slipped on a pair of gold Tom Ford sandals, added a dainty anklet, dabbed on a little lip gloss, and sprayed myself with Tom Ford's Lost Cherry before preparing to head downstairs. Banks was already waiting outside my room, dressed in black swim trunks and a crisp white t-shirt that hugged his chest just right.

He didn't say much at first, just looked at me as I looked at him.

"You good?" he asked.

I nodded. "Are you?"

He stared at me for a moment then exhaled and gave me a small nod. "Yeah. I'm good."

I smiled before Banks grabbed my hand. We headed out to the pool together, walking side by side through the house and into the backyard. The sun was shining down over the beautiful blue water, and the landscaping around the pool was ridiculous – lush greenery, stone paths, tall hedges for privacy, the whole nine. It was the kind of backyard most people only saw in magazines.

I dipped my toes into the water and smiled at the water's perfect temperature. Banks pulled his shirt over his head and tossed it onto a lounge chair. He got into the pool, and I followed right after, taking off my dress and leaving on nothing but my bra and panties. We swam in silence for a bit, just floating, occasionally brushing past each other. After a while, Banks swam to the edge, rested his arms on the ledge, and looked over the yard.

"I should throw something on the grill," he said, wiping water from his face.

I smiled, running my fingers through my wet hair. "You know what? That sounds like a plan."

He turned his head to look at me. "You tryna help?"

I swam over and wrapped my arms around his shoulders from behind. "I'll season the meat; you grill it."

He gave a low chuckle. "Sounds like a plan."

We got out of the pool, water dripping onto the stone patio. I wrapped myself in a towel, and we walked into the house together. Banks opened the fridge and started pulling out all the things we would need.

"I'm gonna go light the grill," he said, placing everything on the counter.

"Go ahead. I got this part," I said, grabbing the seasonings from the cabinet.

Banks glanced at me, smiling, before headed out to the patio. I unwrapped the steaks, washed them, and rubbed them down with olive oil first, then I massaged in sea salt, cracked black pepper, garlic powder, smoked paprika, and a little thyme. Once that was done, I began cleaning and cutting red potatoes. I seasoned them with rosemary, oil, and salt before wrapping them tightly in foil. The corn didn't need much, just butter and a dash of Cajun seasoning. Once I was done, I washed my hands and headed to the liquor cabinet. If we were barbecuing, cocktails were non-negotiable. I grabbed the bottle of tequila, a bag of limes, some agave syrup, and a shaker.

Ten minutes later, I walked outside with two icy Paloma cocktails in hand. Banks was at the grill, focused and fine, shirt still off, and a pair of tongs in hand. I handed him his drink, and he took a sip, nodding in approval.

"Thank you," he said, raising an eyebrow.

"You're welcome. I figured we needed some drinks."

We stood together on the patio, sipping our drinks and talking for a while. I went back inside to toss together a salad. I mixed together spring mix, arugula, cucumbers, cherry tomatoes, red onions, avocado, and cheddar cheese, all drizzled with a honey balsamic vinaigrette I found in the fridge. By the time I came back outside, Banks was plating everything.

Two thick steaks rested on a wooden board, perfectly grilled with dark sear marks. They looked delicious, and I couldn't wait to cut into it. The potatoes were steaming, the corn golden and glistening with extra butter on top. We brought everything over to the outdoor table under the pergola. Banks poured another round of drinks, and we sat in the shade, eating and laughing, our earlier tension slowly melting under the warmth of the day.

"This is nice," I said, cutting into my steak. "You know I'm still mad at Kyrie," I spoke honestly.

Banks looked up at me. "Why? Fuck that nigga."

"Because he put me in this position. And now, even though I'm trying to have a good day, he's still in the back of my mind."

Banks didn't say anything for a second, just leaned back in his chair and stared at me. "You don't owe him anything," he said finally. "Don't let him take space he don't deserve. Like I said, fuck that nigga."

I nodded slowly. "You know what? You're right. Fuck that nigga."

His eyes locked with mine. "I know."

We finished eating as the sun started to dip lower in the sky, painting the yard a golden orange. Afterward, Banks cleaned up the grill while I rinsed the dishes and placed them in the dishwasher. Once everything was all cleaned, we went back outside. We laid on a lounge chair together, our legs tangled, his hand resting on my thigh.

The night had settled over the house like a velvet curtain, the moonlight casting a silver glow over the entire backyard. The soft night breeze kissed my bare thighs. I rested my head on Banks' bare chest. My fingertips traced his tattoos as I watched the stars dance in the sky.

Banks cupped my jaw in his hand and tilted my head up. "You wanna go inside?"

"Nah, I'm good right here."

"Okay, if you say so."

Banks gently moved me off his chest, scooting to the side before lying me back onto the lounge chair. Looking down at me, he slipped off my panties and unhooked my bra, dropping them where he stood. He kneeled in front of me, running his hands up my thighs. He pressed a kiss to my inner thigh then another higher up. His hands spread my legs apart slowly.

He dipped his head and buried his mouth between my thighs, licking slowly, savoring every drop of my juices as they rained down into his mouth. His tongue moved in slow circles, his lips sealing around my clit and sucking with just enough pressure to make me whimper. I gripped the arms of the lounge chair, hips jerking up on their own, the wet heat of his mouth setting my nerves on fire. My breaths turned into shallow gasps, my chest rising and falling like waves crashing with each stroke of his tongue. He licked deeper, the tip of his tongue moving rhythmically while he moaned.

I came hard, my back arching off the chair as I moaned loudly. He stood up slowly, licking his lips, his eyes dark and focused. Then, he pulled his swim trunks down and let them fall. My mouth watered at the sight of him already thick and standing at attention. He climbed onto the chair, lifting me effortlessly and turning me over until I was on my knees, ass up, face pressed to the lounge cushion.

"You wanted to be outside?" he asked, voice oozing with passion. "Let's see how loud you can get under these stars."

I felt him slide the head of his dick between my slick folds, teasing me with slow strokes before easing inside inch by inch. My eyes rolled into the back of my head.

"B-Banks," I moaned.

He gripped my hips before smacking my ass. "You feel that?" he whispered. "You want this dick?"

"Yes, Banks. I want this dick."

"Show me."

His strokes got deeper as I clenched my pelvic muscles and moved my hips in slow circles. The chair creaked under our movements, and every thrust knocked the breath from my lungs. His hand snaked around to my throat, pulling me up against him while he fucked me from behind.

He bent me forward again, one hand at the small of my back while the other slapped my ass hard enough to leave his print. He fucked me harder, sweat glistening on his chest, his abs flexing with every stroke. The sounds of skin slapping and our moans were the only noises being heard. I came again, my walls clenching him so tight he groaned.

"Nah, not yet," he said, pulling out.

He turned me over, climbed on top of me, and slipped back in, this time staring down into my face as he started moving again.

"I want you looking at me when I cum. I want you to remember who got you screaming like this."

He reached down, thumbing my clit, and the orgasm that hit me then was blinding. I cried out his name, dug my nails into his shoulders, my body shaking uncontrollably. Banks cursed, slammed into me three more times, then buried his face in my neck as he spilled into me with a guttural moan.

We laid there for a moment, catching our breath, the night wrapping us in warm silence. Banks kissed my forehead, pulled out slowly, and laid beside me on the lounge chair, pulling my naked body into his.

"Damn," he murmured.

I smiled, still dazed. "Told you I wasn't ready to go inside yet."

He laughed before placing a kiss on my forehead. Banks took my hand, helping me to my feet as we walked inside the house. We walked up the stairs, and Banks led me to his bedroom. We showered together before getting in bed, spending the rest of the night in each other's arms.

Chapter Seventeen

BANKS

I woke up before the sun had even made its way over the trees. The house was quiet, still. But my world wasn't because Braylen was lying right next to me. Her body was turned toward me, her breathing soft and even. She looked peaceful lying there without a care in the world. God only knew what was really going through her mind.

I'd been through too much to believe in love at first sight, but this woman had a hold on me that I hadn't felt in all my years. I watched her chest rise and fall for a moment, my thoughts heavy. I only had two more days with her. Two more days until our deal was up. Two more days before she might walk away from me and back to the same man who handed her over like a car title, like she was something to be traded. That shit ate me up. I didn't want to think about it anymore. Not when she was lying here next to me.

I slid out from under the covers and eased my way between her thighs. I pushed the blankets back slowly, careful not to wake her just yet. Her legs shifted a little, her thighs parting naturally, like her body already knew what was coming. I kissed the inside of her thigh, then higher, until my lips hovered right over her soft, glistening center. Her scent pulled me in, sweet and faintly addictive, like the first inhale of something forbidden. I ran my tongue between her folds, slow and deliberate. She shifted again, a quiet moan escaping her lips. I grinned against her heat.

"Mm," she sighed, still not fully awake.

I licked her again, this time circling her clit with my tongue before sucking it between my lips. Her body jerked slightly.

"Banks..." she whispered, her voice thick with sleep.

"Good morning, baby," I murmured against her. "I missed the taste of you."

She arched her hips, pressing herself into my mouth like she needed it – like I was the first thing she craved in the morning. I kept going, switching between soft strokes and firmer pressure. My hands gripped her thighs, keeping her open for me, guiding her movements as I buried my tongue inside her. She was already so damn wet.

Braylen's fingers twisted in my locs, her breath catching in her throat. "Oh, my God, Banks!"

I looked up briefly, watching her eyes flutter open, her mouth slightly parted. She met my gaze, her body trembling beneath my tongue.

"You like waking up like this, huh?" I asked, dragging a finger through her slick heat and pressing it inside.

She nodded, her head falling back against the pillows. "Yes, baby, don't stop."

I wouldn't have even if she begged me to. I needed to taste her. Needed to feel her legs wrapped around my head like this. Her thighs tensed, her hips grinding against my face. I added another finger, curling them just right while my tongue flicked across her clit again and again. She came with a soft cry, her legs shaking around me as her orgasm hit. I stayed there, holding her through it, licking her slower now but never stopping. I kissed my way back up her body, my chest pressing against hers, our skin warm and damp.

"Morning," I whispered against her lips.

She blinked up at me, still dazed. "That's how you wake people up now?"

I smiled. "Just you."

We kissed slow, like we had nowhere to be, and for a while, we didn't. I pulled her on top of me, letting her straddle my hips. I loved seeing her like this – naked, flushed, and confident. She leaned down and kissed me again, her hands resting on my chest.

"You tryna start some shit before breakfast?" she asked.

"Nah," I said, running my hands down her waist. "Just making sure you know how much I want you."

She looked at me for a moment, and something passed between us – something unspoken but heavy as hell. I knew she felt it just as I did. I sat up and pulled her closer, wrapping my arms around her. "You know I meant what I said, right?"

"About what?"

"About you not going back to him. I don't care what deal he made. I'm not giving you up."

Braylen didn't respond right away. She pressed her forehead against mine, her breath soft against my lips.

"I never asked you to fight for me," she said quietly.

"I know," I whispered. "And I'm not gon' have to. You feel the same thing I feel. Just like that nigga gave you up so easily for a week, he can give you up for life. You mine, Braylen. I'm stakin' claim on that. And that's just what it is."

We stayed like that for a while, her arms around my neck, my fingers tracing the curve of her spine. The sex that followed was slow and deep – different from any other time we'd been together. She took her time riding me, her hips moving like she knew this moment mattered – the same way I did. She kissed me through it, held my face in her hands like I was something fragile. I never felt fragile until her. I never felt like anything could break me until the thought of her leaving did.

Afterwards, we laid tangled in the sheets, her head on my chest, my arms around her waist. I didn't want to let go. I thought about Kyrie and all the shit he'd done. I thought about how he looked standing at my front door with a duffel full of cash, trying to buy her back like it was that simple. Braylen wasn't a transaction. She wasn't a debt to be paid off. She was mine now, and that was something he would have to deal with.

I ran my fingers through her curls, kissing the top of her head. "You hungry?"

She smiled against my chest. "Starving."

I kissed her once more before sliding out of bed and heading for the bathroom. Once I relieved myself, I wrapped a towel around my waist and made my way back to my room to call Marcus. I told him to make something special. I wanted everything to be perfect – pancakes, eggs, fruit, bacon, fresh juice. The works. I even asked him to make one of those sweet peach mimosas she liked.

After showering, I went down to grab the breakfast tray and brought it back upstairs, setting everything up on the table near the balcony in my room. I placed a single white rose in a slim vase, lit a candle, and opened the curtains, so the morning light streamed in. She came out of the bathroom wearing one of my tees, her skin glowing, her smile soft and bright.

"What's all this?" she asked.

"Breakfast," I said. "You earned it."

She walked over and sat down, eyes widening at the spread. "Damn, you didn't have to do all this."

"I wanted to."

She picked up a strawberry and took a bite, her eyes never leaving mine.

"I'm not used to this," she said softly. "Being treated like this."

"Get used to it," I said. "Because if I have my way, this will be your life every day."

She blinked, surprised. But she didn't argue. She just smiled. We ate slow, talking about nothing and everything. After breakfast, I took the dishes back down to the kitchen. I could have had Marcus come get them, but I chose to do it myself. When I got back upstairs, we decided to get dressed for a morning walk on the trail behind my house. It was shaded, private, and wound through tall trees and thick brushes.

Braylen walked to her room, and when she returned a few moments later, she was in a fitted black tank top that clung to her curves and a pair of high-waisted, gray leggings that hugged her hips just right. She tied her curls up into a loose bun and threw on some black sneakers and gold hoops, keeping it casual but still looking fine as hell. I kept it simple in a black, Nike Tech hoodie with matching joggers and black Air Maxes.

We headed out the back gate, walking side by side down the trail, the morning sun streaming through the trees as we walked. The gravel shifted under my shoes as we stepped onto the trail. Early sunlight bled through the trees in golden beams, and the air was thick with the scent of pine, soil, and morning dew. I stole a glance at Braylen walking beside me, and for a second, everything around us faded into background noise.

"You walk this trail often?" she asked, stepping over a root with a little bounce in her step.

"Nah., I had it cut a couple years ago, but I never really used it like that."

"So, why now?"

I paused and looked over at her. "Because you're here."

She didn't respond right away, just kept walking with a small smirk tugging at her lips. The trail curved deeper into the woods, and the deeper we went, the quieter it got. The sound of the city faded behind us. All we could hear were the rustle of the trees, the whisper of birds, and our own breath.

"Last night was different," she spoke suddenly. Her voice was soft, like she was afraid of breaking whatever moment we were in.

I nodded. "Yeah. It was."

She looked over at me then. "I know I said I'm here until Monday. And I meant that. But it's... it's been a lot."

I let out a breath and nodded again. "I know."

"I didn't expect it to feel this real," she confessed.

My jaw tightened. "Because it is real, Braylen. It's been real from the moment you stepped foot in my house. Probably even before that." I stepped in close, lowering my voice. "I don't want you wondering anymore. I want you knowing. I want you choosing me, not feeling stuck between loyalty and happiness."

Her eyes glossed over, but she blinked the shine away before it turned into anything more. I lifted her hand, kissing her knuckles slow. "This ain't just a game to me. You're not some prize I'm tryna win from Kyrie. You matter to me."

"I didn't think you'd care that much."

"I didn't think I could either."

She gave me a small smile then started walking again. I followed her, keeping up with her pace. We came across a small wooden bench I had built into a clearing. It overlooked the small creek that ran through the woods. The water sparkled under the sunlight, moving slow and soft over the rocks. She sat down first, crossing one leg over the other, and I sat beside her.

"I used to come here," I spoke. "Before the money. Before every-thing. When I needed to clear my head, this is where I would come."

"You built all this?"

"Hired some people to make it clean, but yeah. The trail was always here. Just needed some clearing up. All this is my land."

Braylen turned toward me. "You really want me to stay?"

"I never wanted you to leave."

"But you knew I was married when you took me."

"I didn't take you, Braylen. He gave you to me like you was some fucking pawn. And yeah, I went along with it. At first. But this? What we have now? That ain't something you can buy or negotiate."

She went quiet again, watching the water. "Did it ever occur to you," she said finally, "that I might've needed you too?"

My chest tightened at that because I'd been so focused on what I felt, what I wanted, I hadn't really stopped to think about what she might've been carrying.

"I'm sorry," I said. "For how it all started."

"I'm not," she whispered.

The silence after was thick and warm, not awkward at all, just two people finally starting to see each other without anything else in the way. We stood and kept walking. We passed wildflowers growing in patches along the trail. I picked one, some purple thing with a soft stem, and handed it to her without saying anything. She looked surprised, but she took it and held it in her hand as we walked. The trail looped back toward the house, and I could see the gates in the distance.

"Two more days," she said.

"Two more days to decide?"

"Two more days until I stop pretending I don't already know."

I looked at her then. "And what do you know?"

She stopped walking again, turned toward me, and slid her arms around my waist. "That I've never felt safer than I do when I'm with you. That even though this all started the wrong way, it feels more right than anything ever has. That maybe, just maybe, I was meant to end up here."

I pulled her in close, burying my face in her neck. Her scent, her warmth, grounded me in a way nothing else ever had – not money, not status, not fear.

"I want you," I said, lips brushing her skin. "Not just in my bed. But in my life. Wherever I go, I want you with me."

"I want you too."

We walked back to the house slowly. I didn't want the moment to end. Didn't want the peace of the woods to dissolve behind those tall iron gates. I knew now that she wasn't just something beautiful that I wanted to hold onto. She was the piece I didn't know was missing until I had it. I wasn't about to let her slip through my fingers.

As soon as we got back into the house, Braylen headed upstairs to freshen up, and I stayed in the living room for a minute. I pulled out my phone and dialed Sabrina's number. It rang once before she picked up.

"What up doe?"

"I need you to bring something over," I said, cutting to the point.

She didn't ask what. She knew me too well for that. "For you and Braylen?" she asked.

"Yeah. We stepping out tonight."

There was a pause on her end, just long enough to smirk through the phone. "One of *those* nights?"

I grinned. "Exactly."

"Say less. I'll be there in thirty."

I ended the call and slid the phone back in my pocket, leaning back on the armrest of the couch. Tonight wasn't about flexing. It wasn't about being seen. It was about showing Braylen something different – something unforgettable. If I only had two days left with her, I was going to make every second count.

Chapter Eighteen

BRAYLEN

The hot water beat down on my skin like a slow, steady drum, rinsing away the sweat from our walk and the tension I hadn't realized I was holding onto. My muscles were still throbbing from the trail, but it wasn't in a bad way. It was like my body had finally exhaled after holding its breath for days. Walking with Banks, talking, laughing, watching how the breeze teased the edge of his shirt, it was everything I didn't know I needed. There was something different about him today – softer, quieter maybe – but still intense in that way that made you feel like you were the only person in the world when he looked at you.

I tilted my head back under the stream, letting the warmth ease the last of the ache from my shoulders. My mind wandered as I thought about Banks again. The same man who scared most people silent, who could make a room shift just by stepping into it, yet when we were on that trail, his hand brushing against mine, he felt safe.

When I finally stepped out, the bathroom mirror was fogged up completely. I wiped it clean with the edge of my towel and caught my reflection. My skin was flushed, my hair damp and curling slightly at the edges. I wasn't used to wearing wigs, and I was ready to take it off. However, I knew Banks liked it.

I wrapped myself in another towel and walked out into the bedroom, not expecting to find Banks inside my room. He was sitting on the edge of my bed, arms resting on his thighs, phone in his hand like he'd just finished a call. He looked up the moment I entered, and his eyes roamed over my body.

"Hey," I said softly, caught off guard but not uncomfortable.

He smirked, that slow curl of his lips that always made my stomach dip. "You look good wet."

I rolled my eyes but smiled anyway. "You always this charming?"

He stood and walked toward me, his steps unhurried, his gaze never leaving mine. "Only when I'm looking at you."

That made my chest tighten. I was still clutching the towel around me, still slightly damp, and suddenly feeling very aware of every drop of water sliding down my skin under his stare. He stopped a few inches away, and his voice dropped just slightly when he spoke again.

"Ayanna's coming to do your hair. We're going out tonight."

I blinked. "Out? Out where?"

He didn't answer right away. He just leaned in, kissed my cheek so gently it felt like a whisper, and then said it again, this time more deliberate. "We're going out."

Then, he turned and walked out of the room, leaving me standing there in my towel, heart pounding, wondering what the hell that meant and why it thrilled me so much.

An hour later, Ayanna walked through the door like a storm, dressed in all black, trailed by her team carrying sleek, black cases and ring lights. She looked me up and down with a sharp grin. "It's nice to see you again, Braylen."

I laughed lightly. "It's nice to see you again too."

Ayanna's grin widened. "Banks told me it was one of those nights. When Banks says that, you let me work, sis. You about to shut the entire city down."

"What does that even mean?"

"You will see tonight. That's not for me to tell you."

She wasted no time getting started. I sat down in front of the vanity while her assistants set up around us. A warm towel was placed around my shoulders, and Ayanna ran her hands through my hair, assessing it like a canvas. "We're going sultry. Something that says I'm not just his, I'm the one he can't live without."

She blew my hair out smooth before touching up any parts of the lace that weren't perfect. She then pressed it silky straight with a middle part so sharp it could cut glass. Once it was laid, she added soft waves toward the ends, giving it body. She brushed the waves out with a boar bristle brush until they cascaded over my shoulders in perfect, dark layers. Then, she tucked one side behind my ear and slid in a single diamond-encrusted hair pin.

Next came the makeup. The makeup artist started with my skin, smoothing on a hydrating base and a pore less primer. She used a full-coverage foundation that melted into my complexion like a second skin and expertly sculpted my cheekbones with a warm contour that made my face look chiseled and feminine. She brushed a bronzy glow across the high points of my cheeks and added the faintest peach blush for color.

My eyes were next. That was where the sex came in. She used deep matte browns and inky blacks to smoke out the corners, blending them into a flawless gradient that made my almond-shaped eyes look wicked and mesmerizing. A shimmer of gold was pressed into the center of my lids, catching the light every time I blinked. Winged liner carved my eyes into something deadly, and she added a thick set of wispy mink lashes that curled up toward my brows, making my stare impossible to look away from.

She filled my lips in with a dark wine-colored liner then painted them in a soft matte nude that made them look full, kissable, and utterly decadent. She dusted a hint of highlighter along my cupid's bow and stepped back with a proud nod.

"Damn," she said. "If Banks could breathe before, he won't be able to after this."

I looked in the mirror and barely recognized myself. It wasn't because I didn't look like me but because this was the version of me I'd always wanted to see – the woman I was becoming before I met Kyrie.

Ayanna gave my shoulder a squeeze. "Let him take you out and show you off, Braylen. Tonight, you're the fantasy."

Looking at myself in that mirror, I believed her. As Ayanna put the finishing touches on my hair, the door creaked open, and Banks stepped inside with a smile. He held a garment bag in one hand, and I could tell by the way he stared at me that he was pleased with my look.

"Damn, you look…" he trailed off, searching for words. "You look incredible, Braylen."

I gave him a little smile, trying to hide my nervousness. I didn't know where we were going, but his reaction made me feel like I was walking into something I might not be so ready for. He approached the vanity and held out the garment bag. "Sabrina dropped this off for you. Put it on. We're leaving soon."

Without a second thought, I reached for the bag, my fingers brushing his as I took it. I could feel the anticipation crackling in the air. I wasn't sure what to expect from tonight, but I had a feeling Banks was planning something intense. When I unzipped the bag, my breath hitched. The outfit was sexy, revealing, and everything I never thought I'd wear. It was a black, corset-style bodysuit made from a combination of satin and lace that exposed just the right amount of skin. The top was structured with molded cups that pushed my breasts up, giving them an exaggerated, push-up effect. It was laced up tightly at the front, revealing a deep plunge that showed off more than I was used to showing.

The fabric shimmered under the light, and the lace-trimmed edges gave it a delicate but sensual look. The bodysuit clung to my waist, accentuating every curve and giving me a flawless hourglass shape. The bottom portion was sheer black lace, the fabric so light and barely-there that it felt almost like a second skin. The lace disappeared between my legs, and the front was cut high, showing off the tops of my thighs while leaving little to the imagination.

A black choker with a silver clasp finished off the outfit. The entire look was provocative and bold, not something I would usually wear, but I couldn't deny how sexy it made me feel. It made me feel like I was going to dominate whatever night Banks had in mind. I turned to Banks, who was still standing near the door, his gaze locked on me as I held up the outfit.

"You want me to wear this out?" I asked, trying to sound casual. I had no idea where we were going or what the hell was happening, but something told me this night would be unlike anything I'd ever experienced.

"Trust me," Banks said, voice low, his lips curling into a smirk. "You're gonna look even better in it. Go ahead and put it on. We're not gonna be late."

The edge to his voice left little room for argument, so I nodded, and without saying another word, Banks walked out of my room, I slipped into the outfit. It fit like a glove. The tightness around my waist gave me an extra sense of control, while the lace and satin hugged my curves in all the right places.

As I stepped into the foyer, I was immediately struck by Banks' presence. He was standing near the door, waiting for me. The moment my eyes met his, I couldn't help but be captivated by the way he looked. Every inch of him exuded power and dominance. He was wearing an expensive black suit, tailored perfectly to his body, the fabric sleek and polished. What really stood out though was the fact that he was wearing no shirt underneath. His bare chest was on full display, muscular and ripped with tattoos snaking down both arms, chest, and neck. I couldn't help but stare at the intricate artwork etched into his skin, each piece telling its own story.

His jewelry was subtle but undeniably luxurious. Gold chains were draped around his neck, and a watch was on his left wrist that gleamed even in the dim light of the foyer. As I approached, he gave me a slow once-over, and I could feel the weight of his gaze on me, his approval written all over his face. There was no hiding the way he looked at me, and it made me feel like I was the only person in the room, even if we were in a room full of people.

"You look stunning," he said, his voice low, full of appreciation. I gave him a small smile, though I could tell he was already pleased with the way I looked. "You're perfect," he added, his tone leaving no room for argument.

I nodded, my throat a little dry. "Thank you," I whispered, my eyes flicking to his bare chest once more.

Banks reached out and gently took my hand, pulling me toward him. "Let's go. It's time."

He led me out of the house, and we walked down the steps to the waiting SUV. Zeek, who was already behind the wheel, nodded as we approached. He opened the door for me, and I climbed inside, my nerves spiking a little more as I realized I was heading into unknown territory. Banks climbed in beside me, the door closing with a soft thud behind him. He didn't look at me immediately. Instead, he leaned back in his seat, staring out the window of the SUV.

"Where are we going?" I asked, my voice laced with curiosity.

He turned to face me, his eyes dark and intense. "You'll see," he said simply, his hand reaching over to find mine. He squeezed it gently, and I could feel the warmth of his touch spreading through me. "Trust me."

His words were both reassuring and mysterious, and I couldn't help but wonder what he had planned. Something told me that whatever it was, it was going to be more than I was prepared for.

After a short drive through the city, the SUV slowed, and we pulled up in front of a building. It was a sleek, modern structure, located in a quieter part of downtown. The exterior of the building was black glass, almost reflective, with sharp, clean lines, and a sleek, metallic sheen. Other than that, there were no neon lights or even a sign that read the name of the building. It looked more like a private club or some kind of secret venue.

"Where are we?" I asked, trying to get a better sense of where we were. I had no idea what kind of place this was and didn't want to be too surprised when we walked inside.

Banks didn't answer immediately. He was already opening the door for us to walk inside. I hesitated for only a second. He gave me a small, knowing smile, that same confident look he always wore. "Come on," he said softly, pulling me inside the building.

We walked inside the double doors and down a long hallway toward another door. As we reached the door, a man in a sleek, black suit greeted us with a nod, opening the door for us to enter. The moment we stepped inside, the atmosphere changed entirely. The dim lighting, the smooth sound of music in the background, it all felt like stepping into another world. I knew this wasn't just some bougie lounge or private club like I'd imagined. This was something else. This shit looked wild as hell, and I wasn't even sure why Banks would know about this place.

The air was thick with perfume, smoke, and sex. Deep red lighting soaked every surface, casting a sultry glow over the walls and floors. The music was slow, dark, and pulsing. It wasn't loud like a club but low and sensual, like a secret being whispered between strangers. Everywhere I looked, there were bodies – moving and touching one another in ways that should have been kept behind closed doors.

There were velvet couches pushed against mirrored walls where people were lounging. Some were half-dressed and others completely naked, sipping champagne while hands wandered between thighs or up shafts. Others were dancing in the open floor space, but it wasn't the kind of dancing you saw at parties. A woman in nothing but a leather harness was pressed against a man in a suit, grinding on him like she was trying to pull his soul out through his skin. Another couple was sitting in a corner booth, kissing, but the woman's hand was down his pants, and she wasn't shy about it.

My mouth was dry, and my cheeks were burning already. I'd never seen anything like this in my life. I squeezed Banks' hand instinctively. He looked down at me and smirked, that slow, dangerous smirk that told me he'd been waiting for this moment just to see how I'd react.

"You alright?" he asked, his voice low and smooth like the music coming from the speakers.

"I, um, yeah. Just, damn," I whispered, not even knowing what to say.

He chuckled. "Welcome to the underworld, baby."

His grip on my hand tightened as he guided me farther inside. People were watching us as we walked through the space but not in a judgmental way. They were admiring, assessing us like we were their next proposition. It was like entering a world where the rules didn't apply, where desires weren't just felt; they were lived out loud.

A woman walked past us wearing a see-through gown that shimmered in the low light, her nipples pierced, her hips swaying like she didn't have a care in the world. Another woman crawled on all fours at a man's feet, wearing nothing but a collar and leash.

"What is this place?" I asked under my breath.

Banks leaned down, lips brushing my ear. "It's called Obsidian. This is a private, invitation only club. Everyone here signed up for the same thing, Bray. Freedom without judgment."

My heart was pounding but not just from nerves. There was something intoxicating about the vibe in here. Banks led me to the bar tucked along one side of the room. It wasn't like any bar I'd seen. There was dark wood, gold accents, and soft red lighting beneath the counter. The bartender, a woman in a corset and sheer pants, smiled as she handed two guests their drinks then turned her attention to us.

"What can I get you?" she asked.

"Something strong," I said quickly, needing to take the edge off.

"Same," Banks added.

We ended up with two glasses of bourbon, maybe, or whiskey. I took a sip and welcomed the burn. It steadied me a little, helped me get my footing in a place that felt like it operated on pure fantasy.

"Do you come here often?" I asked, glancing sideways at Banks.

His smile curled. "Not often. But I've been here before."

Of course he had. Banks was the type of man who moved in silence but had access to worlds most people couldn't even imagine. I looked around again, this time slower. The longer I stood in it, the less shocked I felt. The more curious I became. To my left, a man was blindfolded and seated in a high back chair while two women fed him strawberries and kissed down his chest. A few feet away, a group of people surrounded a glass-walled room where a couple inside were putting on a show. In another section, there was a stage with silk ropes hanging from the ceiling and a woman being suspended mid-air, her body moving like art while a man slowly rotated her.

"How do people even end up here?" I asked.

"Connections and reputation," Banks answered. "Places like this don't advertise. You get invited."

"And you thought I was ready for something like this?"

He turned toward me, setting his glass on the bar and placing both hands on my waist. "You don't have to be ready for anything. I brought you here to experience something new, not to throw you into anything you don't want."

I studied his face. He wasn't pushing me. He was simply opening the door and letting me decide if I wanted to walk through it or not. The alcohol warmed my blood, but it wasn't just the drink. It was the energy, the slow, sensual rhythm of the place.

"I just..." I paused. "I've never seen anything like this before."

"I know. That's why I brought you here."

My eyes moved across the room again, stopping when I saw a couple in the far corner. The woman was sitting in the man's lap, her back arched, her head thrown back in pleasure. His hands were on her waist, steadying her as she moved on him, not caring who was watching. My thighs clenched.

"What's happening to me?" I murmured.

Banks smiled again, and this time, it was darker. "You're waking up."

I looked at him. His black suit clung to his strong frame, no shirt underneath, showing all those tattoos I'd already traced with my hands and tongue. The low light glinted off the gold chains around his neck and the thick, gold watch on his wrist. I was still adjusting to the fact that a man like him wanted a woman like me, that he looked at me the way he did, touched me the way he did, protected me, even when I didn't ask for it.

"You're not scared, are you?" I asked him, turning to face him fully.

"Of what?"

"Of... me seeing all this. Experiencing it. What if I want more of it?"

He brushed his thumb along my jaw, his touch gentle but grounding. "No. Because I know the more you taste, the more you'll come back to me for it."

My chest tightened. I should've been scared and overwhelmed. But instead, I was fascinated. Something inside me was stirring, like a match being struck for the first time. We stood there for another few minutes, sipping our drinks, watching the room move around us. Every now and then, I caught someone watching us, men and women alike. Banks commanded attention without even trying, and standing beside him, I was starting to feel the ripple effect of that power.

I noticed a woman looking over at us, sipping from a glass of brown liquor. She wore a red thong that was swallowed up by her huge, round backside. She was topless, showing off her perky breasts. Her chocolate brown skin was smooth, and her short pixie cut framed her face. She walked over to us, her ass jiggling with every step she took. She smiled at Banks first before turning to look at me.

"You are fucking beautiful," she exclaimed. "My name is Sienna. What's yours?" She extended her hand.

"Braylen." I took her hand to shake it.

"I would love for you to come with me," she whispered into my ear.

"As long as he can come too," I replied, pointing to Banks.

"I wouldn't have it any other way."

Sienna licked her lips as she looked over at Banks. She led the way through the crowd and down the hall to a closed door, one of several along the narrow hallway. She opened the door, and the three of us stepped inside. The door clicked softly behind us, shutting out the seductive chaos of the party. The room was drenched in red velvet and was thick with the scent of perfume. Her perfume. A low, black, leather sectional stretched beneath a mirrored ceiling. Candles flickered along the wall, casting a soft golden glow around the three of us.

I sat down first, legs crossing instinctively. I could feel Banks' eyes as they roamed over my thighs. He hadn't taken his eyes off me since we stepped into the room. That energy between us was magnetic. However now, there was Sienna too, and that added a heat that made me feel like I was burning from the inside out. I'd never been with a woman before, but I knew the moment I agreed for us to go into the room with her that it was about to happen.

She poured brown liquor into three glasses and passed one to both me and Banks before taking the last glass for herself. She raised her glass. "To letting go," she spoke, voice sultry and eyes locked on me.

We clinked our glasses. "To letting go," I repeated.

I took a sip. The liquor rolled down my throat and settled low in my stomach. Banks hadn't said much, and I wondered what he was thinking. Sienna placed her drink down and stepped close to him, running a single manicured finger along his chest. He didn't move, just looked at me. It as almost as if he was waiting for permission.

I surprised myself when I nodded. "Touch her," I said softly.

Sienna pressed her body against him, taking his face into her hand before kissing him deep and slow. His hands rested low on her waist, controlled yet respectful, until I stood up and walked over to them. It wasn't out of jealousy because that was not what I felt. What I felt was power – watching them, knowing she couldn't have him unless I allowed it, knowing that he still wanted *me* more than anyone in this room. Shit, in the entire party. I walked over and kissed Sienna softly on the back of her neck.

Banks looked at me, eyes dark with hunger. I touched his chest, slowly sliding his suit jacket off him and revealing his bare chest. Sienna was still kissing him, but now, my hands were on him too. I kissed his neck softly, and he reached his hand around and gripped my ass tightly.

Banks broke his kiss with Sienna before turning around to face me. He looked at me, silently asking me if I was sure about this. Without saying a word, I pulled him into me, placing a passionate kiss on his lips.

Sienna walked around and was now behind me, tracing slow circles on my neck with her tongue while she undressed me.

I moved my hands down Banks' chest, allowing my hands to run over his abs. I stopped at his belt, unbuckling it before unzipping his pants and letting them fall to the floor. Sienna was the next to undress, taking off her thong without even being asked. Banks walked over to the couch before taking a seat as he looked up at us. Sienna walked over to me slowly, taking one of my nipples into her mouth. I gasped at the warmth of her mouth against my skin. I eyed Banks as he watched us. He was hard, and all I wanted to do was get on my knees in front of him. I lowered to the couch with her, and she climbed on top of me, her hand sliding between my thighs. I opened for her without question. Her fingers slipped inside me with ease.

"Damn, you're so wet," she whispered. "You like being watched?"

I glanced at Banks. He was stroking himself now, slow and hard, eyes locked on the two of us.

"Yes," I whispered. "I want him to see me."

She smiled and kissed me again as her fingers moved in slow circles inside of me. I moaned softly. Sienna planted a trail of kisses from my breasts, over my stomach, and down lower until her head rested between my legs. Her tongue massaged my clit as I moaned loudly. She grabbed my thighs, pulling me closer to her, and my moans grew louder.

"Banks," I called out, breathless. "Come here."

He was on me in seconds, kneeling beside me, sucking on my nipples as Sienna licked on my love box. I held his head with one hand and Sienna's with the other. Banks looked up at me, and I pulled him to my lips. We kissed for several moments before he stood to his feet, walking down to join Sienna between my legs. I opened my legs wider for them. Banks placed his head between my legs, his cheek pressed against Sienna's.

Two tongues licking and kissing my clit softly sent my body into an uproar. I wrapped one leg around each of their shoulders, arching my back as they both savored me. When it got to be too much, I reached down and pushed them both away. "I want him inside me," I said to her, voice shaking with lust.

Sienna nodded, licking her lips as if this was something she was waiting to see. Sienna kissed his abs while I kissed his thighs, both of us making our way to his manhood. I stopped for a moment, standing up and stepping back. I watched Sienna take him into her mouth, and the slurping sounds filled the room. I watched them for several minutes before I couldn't take it anymore.

"Move," I spoke as I walked back over to them. She stood up without a word. He was throbbing by the time I climbed on top of him, sinking down onto him in one slow stroke. My moan broke the silence. Sienna kissed me while I moved, her tongue teasing mine as I rode him slow and deep.

Banks' hands gripped my hips, guiding me, groaning beneath me. "Damn, Braylen. This shit feels so good."

Sienna moved behind me then, her hands on my waist, her mouth on my neck. Her breasts pressed against my back while I moved up and down on Banks, faster now, chasing the high that kept slipping from my reach. She pinched my nipples, tugged them just enough to make me cry out.

Banks cursed. "You're gonna make me cum."

I slowed down, rolling my hips in circles. "Not yet."

He grabbed my face and kissed me hard. "Shit!"

Sienna laughed low in my ear. "This is so fucking sexy."

She laid back and spread her legs, fingers already pleasing herself. "Let me watch you finish."

I turned to her, licking my lips. "No... I want to taste you."

She moaned when I got off of Banks and dropped between her legs, tongue exploring her, slowly at first then deeper. I'd never eaten pussy before, but something about it felt good. She gasped and tangled her fingers in my hair, guiding me. Banks moved behind me, slid back inside, and now I was doing both, eating her pussy while he fucked me from behind.

Her thighs trembled. I felt her cum against my mouth, and I moaned. That set Banks off. He pumped into me faster, rougher, until my own orgasm ripped through me like a storm. I clenched around him, shaking, and he growled as he came inside me, grabbing my hips with a force that left marks.

When it was over, the room was quiet except for our heavy breathing. Sienna laid beside me, stroking my hair. "You ever done that before?"

I shook my head. "Never."

She smiled. "Well, you damn sure don't need practice."

Banks leaned in, kissed my shoulder, then whispered in my ear, "You surprised me tonight."

I turned to him, lips still swollen from every kiss, every moan. "Good surprise, I hope?"

"The best."

About an hour later, we had both freshened up, redressed, and were now back in the SUV, heading home. We walked inside and went straight up to Banks' room. We both showered and got into bed. I was so tired when I got under the covers that I was fast asleep the moment my head hit the pillow.

Chapter Nineteen

BANKS

Sunlight cut across the floor in thick, golden strips when I opened my eyes. The scent of Braylen's perfume still lingered in the room like it hadn't moved all night. My muscles ached but in a good way. Every part of me felt spent, satisfied, and still greedy for more. I reached for her, expecting to feel the warmth of her skin tucked against me. But the sheets beside me were cool and empty. I sat up, rubbing the sleep from my face, listening before hearing the running water.

I got up, bare feet silent on the floor, and walked into the master bathroom. Steam rolled out in soft clouds, the glass shower already fogged up. I could see her naked body through the steam, and my manhood instantly jumped.

I opened the door without a word and stepped inside. The heat swallowed me instantly, but it wasn't the water that hit me first; it was her. Her eyes opened slowly, and she looked over her shoulder at me, steam clinging to her lashes, droplets running down her back.

"Good morning," she greeted with a smile.

"I haven't stopped thinking about you since I woke up."

She turned around and damn if that sight didn't just knock the breath out of me. Her body glistened, skin slick and glowing. Her hair was wet, tumbling down her back in dark coils.

"I was thinking about last night too," she murmured, stepping closer. "That was very different from anything I'd ever done."

"Did you enjoy it?" I asked, looking down at her.

She pressed a hand against my chest, slick fingers tracing one of the tattoos inked over my heart. "I did enjoy it. I didn't know I could feel that free and still feel like yours."

That did something to me. Before I could say anything, her mouth was on mine. The kiss was slower than the ones we shared last night but deeper, like she was trying to reach the part of me I never showed anybody. I wrapped my arms around her and pulled her in, letting the water beat down on both of us. Her body fit into mine like it belonged there. My hands roamed her back, her waist, cupping her ass and lifting her just enough to pin her against the shower wall. She gasped as I lowered my mouth to her neck, kissing and biting the spots that made her shiver.

"Banks," she whispered, her fingers threading through my locs. "Don't stop."

I wasn't planning to. I dropped to my knees, my face right between her thighs, letting the water cascade down my back. I kissed her inner thigh, slow and deliberate, and when I finally licked her, she let out a loud moan. I ate her like she was the last good thing in this world – tongue deep, fingers gripping her hips to keep her from sliding down the wall. Her legs trembled. She kept one hand braced above her head, the other twisted in my locs, grinding against my mouth as I pulled every drop of pleasure from her.

I didn't stop until she was shaking from the orgasm that was crashing through her body. When I stood back up, her eyes were glassy, mouth parted.

"Come here," she breathed, pulling me closer.

I lifted her up again, one arm under her thigh, the other braced against the wall. She reached between us, guiding me into her. We both moaned at the same time, foreheads touching as I started to move. The water mixed with sweat. Her arms locked around my neck, legs wrapped around my waist. I fucked her like I was never going to see her again, like this was our last time and she needed something to remember me by. Our bodies slammed together over and over, our wet skin colliding with force. Her nails dug into my back as her moans turned breathless.

I pressed my lips to hers as I dove deeper, her body clenching around me, her legs trembling again. I could feel her cumming as her juices flowed down on my shaft, and I wasn't far behind. I held her tighter as I thrust faster, and with one final moan buried in her neck, I let go. We collapsed together under the water, both of us breathless, holding on like we didn't want to let go. The truth was that I didn't – not now, not tomorrow, and not ever.

We both stepped out the shower and wrapped ourselves in towels before walking back into the bedroom area. I sat on the edge of the bed, and she walked over to me. She wrapped one arm around me while running the other one over my locs. I wanted this forever. I wanted her forever. I hated that I had to think about her leaving, that tomorrow might be the last time I got to wake up with her next to me – the last time I got to make her cum in the shower.

"You okay?" she asked, pushing my head up to face her.

"Yeah," I lied. "Just thinking."

"About tomorrow?"

I didn't answer right away, just continued looking up at her. "Yeah," I finally spoke. "But that's just me thinking. We not talkin' 'bout that shit today though. Today, we stay in our little bubble. Just me and you."

She nodded, eyes still holding questions, but she didn't push. I put on a white beater and a pair of black joggers before pulling out my phone and placing a call to Zeek. I asked him to go pick up some food from my favorite Indian spot. I wanted butter chicken, lamb biryani, naan, and samosa. After that, I had Marcus set up the theater room for the day.

If this was the last full day I had with her, I was going to make sure it mattered. We spent the morning outside. She lounged by the pool with a book while I took a few calls from the crew. I kept my eyes on her the whole time though – watching her legs stretched out in the sun, the way she tucked her lip between her teeth when she was reading something intense. Around noon, the food came. We took it downstairs to the theater room then sat on that massive velvet sectional with trays on our laps and laughter in the air.

"Don't eat all the garlic naan," she warned me, already stealing a piece off *my* tray.

"Should've ordered double, huh?"

"Hell yeah, I gotta dip it in each bite of my butter chicken."

The first movie we watched was *Love Jones*. I'd told Braylen that I'd never seen it, and she made sure that was the first movie we watched. Next was *Poetic Justice*. I'd seen this movie a few times, but it had been a while. I refreshed our drinks before we moved on to the next movie. It was *Set It Off*.

She cuddled up close to me, and I kissed the top of her head, breathing her in. I didn't want her to go. I didn't want to wake up tomorrow and pretend she was just a temporary arrangement, that she was a debt paid and nothing more. The truth was that she was so much more to me. She meant so much more to me. I could spend the rest of my life proving that to her. However, I didn't say a word out loud. Not yet. I needed for Braylen to choose me because I was who she wanted. So, instead, I held her tightly while she turned on the next movie.

"See right here?" she said during *Brown Sugar*. "This the scene that makes women fall in love with Taye Diggs. You wouldn't understand."

"Dude got a low cut and a job. Women go crazy for simple things," I teased, shaking my head.

She smacked my thigh. "He got *emotional intelligence* too!"

"Oh, wow," I said. "Not emotional intelligence. That's your type?"

Braylen leaned her head back, laughing. "What's your type then?"

"Right now?" I pulled her closer. "Caramel skin. Hair pulled back in a ponytail. Wearing my shirt. Sitting next to me and just stole all my food off my plate."

She gave me a look. "That sounds *very* specific."

"Exactly my point."

By the time we got to *Jason's Lyric*, things were quiet. It was getting late, and we were starting to wind down. We were still cuddling and sipping from our glasses occasionally. The screen faded to black, and the credits began scrolling slowly. Braylen was still watching, curled beside me under the plush throw blanket, her body warm against mine. We'd spent the entire day tucked away in here, escaping the world. Between the buttery scent of popcorn, the spicy Indian food, and her laughter echoing through my home, I forgot tomorrow existed.

But then I looked at her. I knew that tomorrow meant time was up. Me watching her walk out that door and back to a man who didn't deserve a second of her time. A man who'd gambled her away like she was just another debt to pay. Fuck that. She wasn't leaving here without knowing who she belonged to, without feeling it one last time.

I shifted slightly, pulling her closer until she was straddling my lap. She blinked, her smile dimming. Her lips parted like she wanted to ask me what I was doing, but she already knew. I wrapped a hand around the back of her neck and pulled her in slow, kissing her softly, letting every unspoken word I had bleed out through my tongue.

Her breath caught, and she melted into me like always. I was already hard beneath her, the friction of her hips rolling just enough to make me groan. I reached down and gripped her ass, squeezing tight before slipping my hands up the back of her shirt. I wanted to feel her skin. I broke the kiss and looked up into her eyes, both of us breathing heavy.

"You know you ain't leaving me, right?" I informed.

She bit her bottom lip. "We'll talk about that tomorrow."

"Nah, we talk now."

My hands slid under her shirt, lifting it off in one slow motion. I kissed along her collarbone, letting my teeth scrape just enough to make her arch.

"You feel that?" I whispered against her skin. "That's mine."

She whimpered when I kissed lower, taking her nipple into my mouth. My hand palmed the other breast, massaging in the same rhythm with my tongue as I sucked harder. Braylen moaned, hips lifting to grind against the bulge in my sweats. She clawed at my shirt until I pulled it off, tossing it onto the floor.

I kneeled between her legs and grabbed her thighs, dragging her to the edge of the seat, so I could taste her. I didn't even bother pulling her panties down. I just moved them to the side and dove in. She cried out, back arching so hard I had to hold her down. My tongue slid through her folds, slow and deliberate, tasting every bit of her before I latched onto her clit. I sucked, circled, then flattened my tongue and dragged it up again.

She was trembling in seconds. "Banks, fuck, I'm gonna cum," she screamed out.

I kept going until she snapped, thighs shaking, hands yanking at my locs as she came hard inside my mouth. I didn't stop until she begged me to. When I stood up, my mouth was glistening with her juices, and my dick was painfully hard. I dropped my sweats and boxers, grabbed her ankles, and pulled her to the edge again.

One deep thrust and I was inside. She cried out again, clawing at the armrest behind her as I pounded into her, slow but deep, making her feel every inch. Her walls clenched around me like she didn't want to let go. I grabbed her chin and forced her to look up at me.

"This pussy mine now," I growled, watching her eyes roll back as I hit that spot over and over. "Yo ass ain't going back."

She couldn't even form words anymore, just moaned and whimpered as I fucked her deeper and harder. I lifted one of her legs, propped it on my shoulder, and dove in with everything I had. The sound of skin slapping and her moans filled the room, making a soundtrack to our own movie.

She came again, her whole body tensing as she screamed my name, clawing at me like she was trying to crawl inside my skin. I didn't stop until I came with her, growling low in her ear, spilling inside her as I held her close, our bodies shaking from the release. I stayed there, buried in her warmth, breathing her in. Because no matter what tomorrow brought, she was mine, and I knew she knew it.

Chapter Twenty

KYRIE

It was six in the morning when I finally walked out of the warehouse, my body dragging. I was dead tired, my feet hurt, and I could barely keep my eyes open. However, none of that mattered. Not today. Today was the day my wife was coming home to me. I'd been out for hours, working my magic at the casino. Fifty-two thousand, three hundred and some change. That was how much I walked out with. We'd hit the casino hard, counting cards and shifting tables. Vic's training was paying off, and it felt good to win – but not as good as the thought of finally seeing Braylen walk through that door. That was what had my heart racing, not the money.

I could've gone home and crashed like the rest of the crew. However, sleep wasn't on my mind. I hadn't had her in an entire week. I hadn't even spoken to her since the day she left. I was kicking myself for even doing that shit, offering her up as payment. Every day that passed without her, I regretted it more. Now today, I had the chance to fix it, to bring her home right and change our relationship for the better.

From this day forward, I was going to make sure that she saw the effort I was going to put in, not just my words or my promises. From here on out, I was putting action behind that shit, and she was going to see it.

Remembering what happened the last time I went to Kroger with a large amount of money, I hit Walmart. It was damn near empty, which made it feel like the store was mine. I pushed a cart down the aisle with one hand while the other scrolled through recipes on my phone. I was no chef, but I knew how to put a few things together. I grabbed eggs, thick-cut bacon, fresh strawberries, and some croissants I'd never even tasted before, but they looked good in the picture. I wanted it to look like something off Pinterest. She deserved that plus more.

I hit the floral section next. Most of the bouquets were basic, but I found some white lilies and red roses mixed together. I grabbed two of those. Then, I saw some candles, lavender and sandalwood. I grabbed a few of those too. I was gonna set the whole kitchen up like it was a five-star restaurant. I wanted her to see me trying. I knew this was something she would appreciate.

In the checkout line, the cashier was a short, old lady with kind eyes. She looked up at me with a smile as she began scanning my items. She didn't say anything though, just scanned everything, bagged it up, and gave me a soft, little smile. Maybe she saw in my face how much I needed this morning to go right. I loaded everything in the car and just sat there for a minute with my hands on the steering wheel. For the first time in an entire week, I was able to breathe. My baby was finally coming home to me.

The sun was starting to rise as I pulled out of the Walmart parking lot, painting the sky in streaks of orange and pink. It was beautiful in a way I hadn't paid attention to in a long time. This morning, everything felt brand new – maybe because it was. This morning was the first day of the rest of my life, the rest of our life together. This was a fresh start, and nothing that happened before today mattered.

I cracked the window and let the early breeze hit my face. My body was worn down, but my chest was light – like hope was sitting in my passenger seat. I couldn't stop smiling. I tapped the steering wheel to a beat that wasn't playing, just something inside of me, something happy.

I was going to show my wife how much I truly loved her. She was the woman of my dreams, and it was time that I started acting like it. I was going to give her the life she deserved. There was no more of her working her fingers to the bone at that damn plant. With all the money I was making now, Braylen would never have to work again. It was time for me to put my baby in her soft girl era. I'd been a damn fool, and I knew it. I was in shit so deep, and Banks offered me a way out. But when I became desperate, I offered up my wife. That was fucked up, and I was going to spend however long it took to prove to Braylen just how sorry I was.

I owed her a real apology, not some quick "I'm sorry." I wanted her to feel it in every word. I wanted her to know I regretted it every single day, that it broke me not hearing her voice or seeing her face. The thought of her fucking Banks ripped my heart in two. But I knew it was my own fault. She wouldn't even be with Banks if it wasn't for me. So, I had to own all that shit, so we could move past it. I had to show her that I was ready to fight for us.

By the time I pulled into the driveway, the sky was full-blown morning. Birds were chirping, singing a song like they knew I was trying to get my girl back. I grabbed the bags from the trunk and headed inside, locking the door behind me. The house was quiet. It didn't feel like a home without her in it. Her laugh, her scent, her little humming when she did her hair in the bathroom, I missed all of it.

I dropped the bags on the kitchen counter and went straight to the bathroom. I needed to wake up a little before I started cooking. Hot water beat down on my back as I leaned against the shower wall, eyes closed, thinking about what I was gonna say. *I was wrong. I let my fear make decisions for me. I forgot who I was, who we were. And I promise you, Braylen, if you come home to me, I'll never gamble with your heart again.* I repeated it out loud a couple times, letting the words roll off my tongue. I meant everything I said, and I prayed Braylen would see that.

Once I was out the shower, I threw on a pair of gray joggers and a fresh tee. I lit a few of the candles in the kitchen. I filled a vase with cold water and arranged the lilies and roses in it, setting them dead center on the table. I cracked eggs into a glass bowl, added a little cream, salt, and pepper. The bacon sizzled in the pan beside me while I sliced up the strawberries and piled them into a fancy-ass glass bowl like I knew what I was doing. I even tried to toast the croissants.

It was shaping up to look like something off one of those cooking shows she used to watch. I didn't even care how tired I was. Every time I looked at that clock ticking closer to the hour, my heart beat faster. Everything in me prayed that she would walk through that door and see what I was trying to be and not just who I used to be.

By the time I stepped back and looked at everything I'd done, I felt a tight pull in my chest. My nerves were starting to get the best of me. I hadn't been this nervous to see Braylen since our first date. The kitchen was glowing with soft candlelight, the scent of lavender drifting through the air and mixing with the warmth of cooked bacon and toasted croissants. I had the table set for two – real plates this time, not paper like I usually used when we ate. Wine glasses, cloth napkins, and silverware were laid out like we were dining in some five-star restaurant.

The flowers set in the middle, full and bold. A mix of white lilies and deep red roses, just how she liked them. I even played a playlist on low in the background – some H.E.R., some D'Angelo, a little Lauryn Hill – because I knew that was what used to get her feeling good. I looked at the time. It was eight fifty-six. She left at nine that morning a week ago. So, I figured maybe that was when she'd come back.

I sat down on the edge of the couch with my phone in my hand, staring at the front door like it would swing open at any second. My leg bounced without me meaning to, and I kept rubbing my palms together like I was trying to make fire. It was nine fifteen now. I was still calm, thinking maybe she just needed a minute. Maybe she just got caught up. I understood that it had to be hard for her. She thought that she was coming back to the same old me, but that wasn't the case.

By nine forty-three and still nothing, my heart started to sink just a little. By ten twenty-seven, I'd already stood up and sat back down three or four times. I checked my phone more than that. There were no missed calls, texts, or notifications. My appetite was gone, and I didn't even want to eat anymore. By eleven ten, I was pacing.

A part of me wanted to call her, just hit her line and hear her voice, even if it was her voicemail again. But something stopped me. That quiet rejection of silence I kept getting every time I tried. That shit did more damage than I liked to admit. Still, my thumb hovered over her name in my favorites. I stared at it, breathing slow. Wondering if maybe Banks had talked her into staying. Wondering if maybe she wasn't mine anymore.

Just when I was about to close the screen, when the fire was damn near gone and I was thinking maybe this whole setup was for nothing, the front door opened, and my entire body froze. I heard keys drop, then light footsteps walking toward me, then I saw her. She was wearing a pair of white slacks that fit her perfectly and a black, lace, corset top. Her hair was weaved down her back in flowing curls, and the gold jewelry she wore looked expensive. I swore, in that second, I forgot how to breathe.

I rushed toward her like a man who'd been crawling through a desert and finally saw water. My arms wrapped around her waist, and I pulled her into me tight, burying my face in her neck. She smelled so good, unlike anything I'd ever smelled on her before. I knew that whatever it was, it was expensive too. She looked nothing like the Braylen that left just a week ago.

I didn't care. I just held her anyway.

"Braylen," I whispered, my voice already cracking. "I'm so sorry, baby. I'm so damn sorry."

She didn't hug me back, but I kept talking. I had to get it out. "I was stupid. I shouldn't have ever sent you to him. I just... I was desperate. But not desperate enough to lose you. I don't wanna live without you, Bray. I swear to God, I'll do whatever it takes to make this right."

She finally pulled back, just a little, and looked at me. That was when I saw it, the look on her face, the one that made my chest go cold. She wasn't crying. She wasn't angry. She was indifferent. Her nose scrunched like the air was bothering her, like being here left a bad taste in her mouth. She looked around the living room like it was unfamiliar or worse, beneath her now.

I blinked, stepping back a bit, trying to keep my voice steady. "I made you breakfast. Come sit with me, baby. Let's eat together and talk."

She didn't answer. She just turned and walked up the stairs. No hi. No thank you. No I missed you too. I stood there in silence, unsure if I should follow her right away or give her a minute. Maybe she needed to decompress. Coming back home after what happened, I knew it would take adjusting.

Five minutes passed, then ten, and I couldn't sit still anymore. I climbed the stairs slowly, my heart thudding hard against my chest. I didn't knock. I just pushed our bedroom door open. Braylen was standing at the dresser, pulling open drawers. She already had her travel bag on the bed, half full. But what stopped me was the sight of her care-

fully placing the velvet box from the back of the closet into her purse –
the one that held her grandmother's jewelry.

I froze in the doorway. "Braylen... what are you doing?"

She didn't answer right away. She kept her back to me, her hands
gentle and precise as she gathered papers from the top drawer, ones I
knew were her birth certificate, her passport, and a few other important
documents.

"Bray?" I stepped inside. "Talk to me."

She finally turned, her face calm but her eyes colder than I'd ever
seen. "I'm getting my things."

Her voice sliced through me like a blade. "For what?" I asked, stepping closer, my throat tight. "You just got home."

She didn't flinch. "This isn't my home anymore."

My knees almost buckled. I stared at her, mouth open, breath
trapped in my lungs. "Braylen, no. Don't do this. You came back, which
means something, right?"

She looked at me for a long second and then shook her head. "I
came back to get what's mine. That's all."

"All of this is yours. I'm what's yours. We have an entire life
together. I know it's been rocky, but that's what I want to talk to you
about. We can fix all this shit. I can take care of you now. You ain't gon'
never have to work at that plant again."

"I don't work there anymore," she spoke, placing the last of the
papers inside the bag.

"Bray, please. I'm your husband."

"Nah, not anymore. I want a divorce."

Her words cut like a knife through my heart. My eyes began to burn
as if tears were about to fall. I looked at her, not believing the words that
left her lips. However, when she zipped the bag, grabbed it, and walked
right past me without saying a word, I knew she was serious. My heart
felt like it had just broken in a million pieces. The hard me was gone.
The moment I heard the front door shut, I fell to the floor and cried.

Chapter Twenty-One

BRAYLEN

It had been a month since I walked out of that townhouse, and I'd never looked back. I had never been happier in my entire life than I'd been this past month. I wake up every morning to peace – the kind that wraps around you and doesn't let go, the kind that smells like Banks' cologne on his pillow and tastes like fresh berries and whipped cream on the breakfast tray he brings to bed. His house was *our* house now, and it felt like freedom – like choosing myself for the first time in a long time.

Banks was everything, and I was so in love. It was wild how fast life could change when you stopped surviving and started living. I see it in my skin, in the way my shoulders don't feel tight anymore. I hear it in my own voice. No more snapping, no more walking on eggshells. Just laughter and true, unapologetic love. Leaving Kyrie was much easier than I thought it would be. The moment I walked inside that sad ass townhome and saw his face, I knew.

The day after I moved in with Banks, I contacted a divorce attorney. Her name is Camille Wright, and from the moment we sat down, she made it clear that I had options. She told me everything I'd need to gather to start the process, and I didn't waste any time. The first step was filing the initial petition for divorce. Camille helped me write my statement and submit it to the county clerk. Since Kyrie and I didn't have kids, the paperwork was already simpler, but I still wanted everything to be done cleanly.

I signed the petition, and we had it served to Kyrie the following day. Camille arranged for a process server to deliver it in person. I didn't ask how he reacted when he got it. I didn't need to because I already knew. Kyrie thought I would never leave him. That was why he treated me the way he did. However, now the joke was on him.

The next step was financial disclosures. I submitted copies of my recent bank statements, tax returns, and the title to my car – everything I owned on paper. Camille was on top of everything, letting me know that Kyrie would have to do the same, and if he acted petty, she would handle it. After that, we'd set a mediation date. But right now? I was focused on healing.

I didn't miss Kyrie, not the version of him I left behind – the man who handed me over like a pawn on a chessboard. I grieved that marriage while I was still in it. Now, I was just grateful I had the courage to leave.

Banks walked in while I was standing at the mirror, brushing out my curls. He slid his arms around my waist from behind and rested his chin on my shoulder, meeting my eyes in the glass.

"You smiling to yourself again?" he asked, that deep voice low and amused.

"Maybe," I said with a smirk.

He pressed a kiss to my neck. "You look good happy."

"I feel good happy."

"Then I'm doing my job."

I laughed and turned around to face him. "You're doing a damn good job."

***

It was one of those perfect Saturdays where the sun was just warm enough, the breeze came through soft and playful, and the pool water glittered like glass. I'd invited Vita over to the house, so she could finally meet Banks. She'd been dying to put eyes on the man I left Kyrie for, the man who now had me glowing like I swallowed the moon. Honestly, I wanted her to see this part of my life, the calming luxury of the *me* I was becoming.

Banks had Marcus put together something light but elegant for lunch – his specialty. We ate by the pool under a wide, cream-colored umbrella. Marcus laid the table with a fresh white linen runner and minimalist gold-trimmed plates. He served chilled cucumber and melon soup in crystal bowls with a dollop of crème fraiche and fresh mint. Then came the main course – seared lemon herb shrimp over a bed of arugula and citrus quinoa, garnished with edible flowers and a drizzle of garlic-lime vinaigrette. On the side were grilled peach crostinis with whipped goat cheese, honey, and crushed pistachios.

Vita and I were on our third round of pineapple basil mojitos, while Banks sipped from a tall glass of strawberry lemonade laced with tequila.

"You know," Vita said, leaning back in her chair with her legs crossed, "I can finally say it, girl. You done upgraded. You went from roaches and ramen to a man who got chefs and marble counters."

Banks chuckled, glancing at her over the rim of his glass. "That's supposed to be a compliment?"

"Absolutely." Vita grinned. "You rich-rich, huh?"

He smirked. "I do alright."

I rolled my eyes and laughed, already tipsy from the drinks. We played music from the Bluetooth speakers tucked into the landscaping, old-school R&B mixed with some new school. Vita danced a little while sitting, waving her hand in the air and singing along to Summer Walker like she was at a private concert. Banks kept looking at me with that soft smile he only gave me when he thought no one noticed, but Vita noticed.

"He in love with you already," she whispered behind her mojito. "Don't fumble, sis."

I grinned and leaned into the back of my chair, the smell of sunblock, grilled peaches, and mojito mint filling the air around me. I felt full in a way that had nothing to do with food. My soul was finally full from the love of a man that I knew cherished me.

A few hours later, Vita was sprawled across the lounge chair, laughing at nothing, her legs dangling over the side like she didn't have a single bone left in her body.

"I swwwearrr," she slurred, lifting her glass and nearly spilling the last drops of her drink, "if I stay here any longer, I'm gonna try to fuck yo man."

Banks barked out a laugh from across the table. "You definitely not stayin' then."

Vita waved him off. "I'm serious. He smell too good. I'm drunk and horny, and I'm not about to disrespect your little fairytale, Bray."

I couldn't do anything but laugh. I knew she wasn't serious, but the look on Banks' face was telling me to get her out of here now.

"I'm callin' Zeek," Banks said, already pulling out his phone. "You ain't drivin', and you ain't stayin'. You gettin' chauffeured like the queen you think you are. You can come pick your car up tomorrow."

"Damn right," Vita mumbled, closing her eyes with a content sigh. "Luxury only."

The next morning, I woke up feeling like shit. My head felt like it had been cracked open with a brick, and every movement made my stomach churn. I barely made it to the bathroom before I was on my knees, dry heaving and sweating like I'd just finished running laps.

Banks stood in the doorway shirtless, rubbing sleep from his eyes. "Damn, baby," he muttered, kneeling beside me and pulling my hair back. "You alright?"

I couldn't even answer. I was too busy throwing up again. He helped me to the sink, rinsed my mouth, and guided me back to bed. I could barely keep my eyes open. He kissed my forehead and tucked the covers over me like I was made of glass. I slept the whole day away. I only woke up for a few sips of water then passed right back out.

The day after that? More of the same. The day after that, I was still throwing up, still exhausted, and now, I couldn't stand the smell of food. Banks was standing in the kitchen, watching me from the island with his arms folded, when it clicked for both of us at the same time.

"Yo," he said slowly, his eyes narrowing, "you think you might be?"

I froze with a glass of ginger ale halfway to my lips.

He was already grabbing his phone to call Zeek. "I'll be back."

I sat on the edge of the tub, staring at the test on the counter. I'd already taken two. Both of them read the same thing. Pregnant. I didn't even realize I was crying until Banks crouched down in front of me and wiped a tear from my cheek.

"Hey," he said softly, his voice thick, "that's a *good* thing, Bray. Right?"

I nodded, the tears still coming. "Yeah, it is. I always wanted to be a mama, and now, I'm about to be."

He smiled the biggest smile I'd ever seen. "You really 'bout to have my baby?"

I nodded again, and he pulled me into his arms, holding me so tight I could feel the beat of his heart against my chest. We stayed like that, sitting on the bathroom floor with two tests between us and a whole new world opening up.

He kissed the top of my head. "We 'bout to start a family."

I had barely slept the night before, too excited, too anxious. It had been a whole week since I found out I was pregnant, and today, I was finally going to see the baby and hear his or her little heartbeat. Hearing the heartbeat would make it real. I kept rubbing my belly like I was already showing, even though I wasn't. That tiny life inside me had already changed everything.

I wanted to look good, even if it was just a routine appointment. I slipped into a cream-colored, body-hugging, maxi dress with short sleeves, soft and stretchy around my stomach. My edges were laid, and my jet-black leave-out was curled into loose, polished waves that brushed my shoulders. I spritzed on my Baccarat Rouge, just a little, not wanting to overdo it. The scent lingered like a kiss in the air. I wanted to smell like I felt, like I was glowing from the inside out. Banks was already downstairs waiting, leaning against the hood of the SUV, dressed down in a black fitted tee, jeans, and clean sneakers. Even casual, he looked like money. He opened the door for me, kissed my cheek, and told me again how proud he was.

"Let's go see our baby," he said, smiling like he'd already claimed it.

The ride to the OB-GYN office felt longer than it was, even with music playing and Banks holding my hand the whole way. I couldn't stop bouncing my leg. My nerves were on fire, and my heart was racing.

Once inside, the front desk nurse smiled at me like she could already tell it was my first time. The waiting room was quiet, the kind of space where you couldn't help but feel hopeful, watching other glowing women – bellies already showing, leaving with ultrasound pictures in their hands. I imagined that would be me in a few months.

When they finally called my name, Banks stood up with me and walked back with a huge smile on his face. He kept rubbing my back while the tech asked me to lie back and lift my dress. My hands were clammy, my stomach fluttering with something deeper than nerves.

The tech smiled. "Let's get a look at your little one."

Then, the cold gel touched my belly, and the wand moved across my skin. The monitor came to life in front of us, and in that instant, there it was – a soft, steady rhythm. It was the heartbeat.

I gasped, my hand flying to my mouth. My eyes filled with tears so fast I couldn't stop them.

Banks reached over and squeezed my hand, his voice tight with emotion. "That's really our baby?"

I nodded, unable to speak, my chest tight with joy. I laughed through the tears, covering my face, overwhelmed in the best way.

"I can't believe it," I whispered. "That's our baby's heartbeat."

Banks leaned in and kissed my forehead then my belly. "Already sounds strong," he murmured. "Just like you."

But then, the tech frowned slightly and tilted the monitor, adjusting something. Her voice was still friendly but curious. "You said you found out last week, right?"

I nodded, wiping my face. "Yeah, just a few days ago."

She smiled gently, still staring at the screen. "Okay. That's what I thought. But you're measuring at about twelve weeks. That's three months along."

Everything in the room slowed. Three months? My heart stopped. I blinked at her, the warmth draining from my face. "Wait, what?"

The tech looked back at me, nodding confidently. "Yeah. Based on the crown-rump length and fetal development, you're measuring at right around the end of your first trimester. Not just a few weeks." She turned the screen again and pointed. "That's a much more developed embryo than what we'd expect at six weeks. This little one's been growing for a while."

I stared at the monitor, at the shape that had been so beautiful just seconds ago. Then I realized that three months ago, I didn't even know Banks. This was Kyrie's baby that was growing inside me. I didn't say anything. I couldn't. I just laid there, frozen under the weight of that truth, Banks still gripping my hand, smiling like his whole world was unfolding in front of him. And just like that, mine cracked wide open.

To Be Continued...

**The Promissory 2
Coming Soon**

Did you enjoy the read?
Let us know how much by leaving us a
review on Amazon and Goodreads.

Other Books By

URBAN AINT DEAD

Tales 4rm Da Dale

The Hottest Summer Ever

Hittin' Licks For The Holidays: Atlanta

Wet Dreams On Lockdown: The Nurse

How To Publish A Book From Prison

How To Invest In The Stock Market From Prison

By **Elijah R. Freeman**

Despite The Odds

Despite The Odds 2

By **Juhnell Morgan**

Good Girls Gone Rogue

Good Girls Gone Rogue 2

By **Manny Black**

Hittaz

Hittaz 2

Hittaz 3

Hittaz 4

Hittaz 5

Hittaz 6

Coldhearted

Coldhearted 2

Coldhearted 3

By **Lou Garden Price, Sr.**

A Holiday Heist

Healing The Heart Of A Detroit Gangsta

By **Kyiris Ashley**

Stuck In The Trenches

Stuck In The Trenches 2

By **Huff Tha Great**

Melted The Heart Of A Menace

Wet Dreams On Lockdown: Lieutenant Grace

By **P. Wise**

Merry Trapmas

By **Mia Sky**

Thug Me The Right Way

By **DiamondATL & Nai**

Wet Dreams On Lockdown: The Counselor

By **Paris Iman**

Wet Dreams On Lockdown: The Male C.O

By **Tamyra Griffin**

Wet Dreams On Lockdown: The Captain

By **TN Jones**

Wet Dreams On Lockdown: The Warden

By **Shawnice**

Atlantastan

Atlantastan 2

By **Chris Green**

IN The Streetz

IN The Streetz 2

IN The Streetz 3

IN The Streetz 4

IN The Streetz 5

By **Tron Hill**

Hittin' Licks For The Holidays: New York

Bandemic

By **Freshh Moneyy**

Coming Soon From
URBAN AINT DEAD

Drill
The Hottest Summer Ever 2
THE G-CODE
Tales 4rm Da Dale 2
How To Build Your Credit From Prison
By **Elijah R. Freeman**

Good Girls Gone Rogue 3
By **Manny Black**

Despite The Odds 3
By **Juhnell Morgan**

Wizdom: Forever Your Gangsta
By **Nai**

This Time Won't You Save Me 3
By **Kyiris Ashley**

Atlantastan 3
By **Chris Green**

IN The Streetz 6
By **Tron Hill**

Bandemic 2
By Freshh Moneyy

www.ingramcontent.com/pod-product-compliance
Lightning Source LLC
Chambersburg PA
CBHW060420310726
48976CB00003B/1130